Cold and Lonely, Lovely Work of Art

S. Anne Gardner

Affinity
eBook Press
NZ
2014

Cold and Lonely, Lovely Work of Art
© S. Anne Gardner 2014

Affinity E-Book Press NZ LTD.
Canterbury, New Zealand

1st Edition

ISBN: 978-1-927282-79-3

All rights reserved.

No part of this book may be reproduced in any form without the express permission of the author and publisher. Please note that piracy of copyrighted materials violate the author's rights and is *illegal*.

This is a work of fiction. Names, character, places, and incidents are the product of the author's imagination or are used fictitiously and any resemblance to actual persons living or dead, businesses, companies, events, or locales is entirely coincidental.

Editor: Ruth Stanley
Cover Design: Irish Dragon Designs

Acknowledgements

The words thank you are so small when there are so many more words that I can express. So many have made this possible and to which I am so grateful. I thank you all, I love you all, I am so grateful to you all.

Lisa, I have no words for the contribution that you make to every word written…

My children, my loves, you are the reason that I was created.

Mel, I am so grateful for all your support, for the advice, the input, the assistance and your friendship. Thank you.

To Ruth, my editor, who somehow understands my silences and my passionate nature and, simply said, makes my work so much better. Thank you.

To Belinda, my dear friend, who has assisted with correcting my Spanish grammar and accents…those accents are enough to drive me crazy. Thank you, my friend.

Always and forever my thanks to all the readers who have taken the time to let me know how much you enjoy my work. Thank you and thank you again for reading my work.

Thank you Mel for the cover.

Dedication

For the love of a woman…my woman.
For Lisa…

Table of Contents

Chapter One

Barbara walked and struggled to breathe. All she knew was that she wanted the distance between where she had been and where she was going to grow and grow and grow. It didn't matter where her steps were taking her.

Barbara hadn't noticed how quickly she was becoming out of place to the area, nor the eyes that had not left her for the last four blocks. Overwhelmed by what she had been told only moments ago, where she was going made little difference. Her mind kept replaying again and again the events that had brought her to this point in her life.

She had walked out of the Newark County Courthouse and turned down a street and just kept walking. The Newark downtown was experiencing a renaissance with the building of the New Jersey Performing Arts Center and with big companies relocating into new headquarters because of tax incentives. Parking was next to impossible so she had taken a cab to her meeting with her attorney, and had planned on taking another home.

The law firm was on the twenty-fifth floor of the office building across from the courthouse, which was connected to the building by a newly built overpass. All the new businesses were bringing in much needed revenue and the areas surrounding the performing arts centers had changed tremendously. Despite the improvements, including a new and more visible police presence, the city was still very much a dangerous one. Now, as Barbara walked, deep in thought, she never noticed as the streets got dirtier and how more and more houses were boarded up.

"Fresh meat," she heard an unsavory voice say, seemingly from nowhere.

Barbara suddenly stopped walking and looked around. For the first time she seemed to realize she had no idea where she was and that she was probably in great danger. She turned and looked in all directions. Her senses suddenly kicked in. No one was visible on the street, there was garbage everywhere, and the houses on either side of her seemed to be abandoned. Her heart began to pound so hard in her chest that she could hear it in her ears. She looked in all directions and was shocked by what she saw. All her fears came to life when two men emerged from the shadows and stopped a mere few feet in front of her.

Barbara froze. Nothing had prepared her for this. She took a step back as fear flooded her face. The two men were unshaven and dirty, and by the expression on their faces it was very obvious what they had in mind.

"Me first," the one to the left said to his partner.

"Why not just take turns? Oh…this is going to be good."

Speechless with fear Barbara turned and began to run. They quickly overtook her and shoved her into an alley, then against a wall. The man in front of her covered her mouth with one hand while the other began to tear the front of her blouse open. His breath and the foulness of his stench assaulted all her senses. She tried to scream as she felt a hand between her legs but couldn't. Horror and terror was mirrored in her blue eyes.

"Animal!" someone growled in Spanish from behind them.

All Barbara saw was the two men being pulled off her. She stood unable to move, frozen with fear.

The two men turned around, prepared to strike at the person who had denied them what they were about to enjoy. When they saw the woman standing behind them they froze as well.

"Taya…she wandered into our pen. She belongs to us." The man that had held her against the wall spoke first, anxiously.

The woman walked slowly up to Barbara, who focused on her. Their eyes locked both questioning.

Barbara stared at the dark-clad woman. "Help me," she said barely above a whisper.

Barbara's blouse was ripped open and Taya could see the breasts that had been covered in the now-torn lace bra.

How exquisite, Taya thought.

As Barbara stood partially naked in front of her, Taya's demeanor completely changed as her eyes went from her breasts to her eyes again. Taya's hand lightly touched the face in front of her in admiration. "Do you want to come with me?"

Barbara nodded quickly as the tears she was holding back spilled over.

"I'm taking her," Taya said, never breaking eye contact with Barbara.

"No! She came into our pen."

Taya turned around and moved to the side before the man closest to her swung at her.

"You must learn to listen," Taya said with a voice as cold as steel before she pulled out a blade that went straight into her attacker's leg.

"Oh, God!" he screamed and held his leg with both hands. Blood oozed out between his fingers and he dropped to the ground.

"God can't help you now," she said coldly.

Taya turned to the other man, who took two steps away slowly.

"Whatever you want, Taya," the other man assured her as he kept backing away.

Taya turned toward Barbara again, who looked totally terrified. This one she would enjoy, Taya told herself and smiled. She was surprised when Barbara came into her arms and held on to her tightly.

For a moment the contact had taken her by surprise and as a result of it Taya's senses were filled with the fragrance and the softness of the woman in her arms. She allowed the embrace long enough to bury her face in the woman's soft, sweet-smelling blond hair.

"I'm sorry," Barbara whispered as she fumbled with her coat to cover her breasts. Her reaction to seeking safety in a stranger's arms made no sense. But, there was something about this woman that on some primal level pulled her to her.

"Let's get off the street," was all Taya said. Barbara looked into the darkest eyes she had ever seen and nodded.

As they walked down the street Barbara could see shadows lurking in the alleys. As she felt the ominous darkness closing in around her she grabbed Taya's arm tighter to her.

Taya looked toward the woman who clung to her for protection and a dark smile appeared on her face for a brief moment. Barbara never saw it. The dark shadows would come out and then back away as they walked past them.

The lamb is clinging to the lion. Taya smiled at the thought.

Barbara followed her rescuer without question into a building. Taya opened a door and walked into an apartment and Barbara walked in behind her.

"Close the door," Taya said as she turned to face Barbara. "Lock it."

Barbara complied then turned around to face Taya once more. Taya noticed how the woman trembled.

"They were going to…" Barbara covered her face and her body shook as she began sobbing.

Taya approached her slowly and stopped barely an inch away, not exactly understanding why she was taking so much trouble with the woman in front of her.

Barbara leaned into the woman who had rescued her from being raped and, more likely than not, had saved her life as well. She cried as she clung harder to Taya.

Taya's arms came up slowly and pulled her closer to her still. Again she felt her senses come alive and she pulled away quickly, trying to deny even to herself the reaction this woman was producing in her.

Barbara looked at her now as she wiped away the tears. "I want to thank you."

"Thank me," Taya said softly, putting some distance between them.

Barbara looked at her for a moment and Taya wondered if she had understood her request. Her request?

"Thank you," Barbara said as a soft smile appeared on her face.

Taya looked at her. Obviously not, she thought to herself sarcastically.

"If you would grant me one more thing?"

Taya raised a brow, laughed and then nodded. She had taken this woman from Jake and Stanley because she wanted her for herself and here she was, not fucking her brains out but agreeing to something she didn't even know yet. This is one for the books, Taya thought.

"If I could use your phone to call a cab?"

"No phone," Taya said as she turned around and started removing her coat.

"Oh?"

"A cab is an oddity here during the day. It would never come into this part of town at night. It's getting dark." Taya lit a cigarette and leaned against the table behind her.

Barbara looked at her in confusion and fascination. There was something dangerous beneath the surface of the woman in front of her. There was also a sensuality about her that seemed to ooze out of her pores. And somehow there was a part that was hiding because surely there was more hidden behind those piercing eyes.

"You are too tempting a prize out there now," Taya said as she exhaled, shaking Barbara out of her thoughts. "In the morning I will take you home." Taya put out her cigarette and walked into another room.

Barbara looked around the apartment, noting that it held only the mere necessities. Spartan almost. It was empty of the usual things—no personal items of any kind, no mementos, no photos. That she could almost understand. But, why no phone? Everyone had a phone in this day and age, didn't they?

"The line keeps getting cut," said Taya as she walked back into the room.

Barbara looked at her questioningly.

Taya looked toward her as she set down two plates on the table. "I figured that was the next question."

Barbara relaxed a little as she saw the smile that now covered the woman's face. Quite suddenly she noticed the beauty of her dark-haired rescuer. "Hope you like pasta." She looked at the woman in front of her and wondered what she was doing living here. There was a strength and arrogance about her that only seemed to accentuate her exotic beauty.

"Yes, thank you," Barbara said as she began to relax some more.

"Take your coat off."

Barbara looked down then back at Taya.

"Did they hurt you?" Taya walked up to her and pulled the coat open, not waiting for Barbara to answer. She then looked up into Barbara's blue eyes. "Just your modesty," Taya said softly in almost a whisper as she looked back down at Barbara's exposed breasts. Her eyes lingered for a moment then looked back up at the frightened woman again. "Come with me."

Taya walked into another room and Barbara followed quietly. She really had no choice at this point. She reasoned that the woman in front of her, up to now, had only been kind; she would have to have faith that the kindness would continue. In her present state of mind that was what she needed to believe.

Barbara walked into a large bedroom. Again she noticed the bareness of the room. The bed was king-sized and looked clean. Next to it was a nightstand with a lamp and a digital clock. This woman obviously only believed in the bare essentials and nothing more, and yet somehow it didn't seem like her.

Taya opened another door, which turned out to be the closet, and pulled out a black T-shirt, holding it up for her to take.

Barbara looked at the shirt then at Taya.

"Thank you." Barbara took the T-shirt. Taya put her hand out again. Barbara seemed confused.

"Your coat." Taya waited for Barbara to take off her mink coat. When Barbara seemed to hesitate she added, "I will hang it up. You will get it back when I take you home tomorrow."

Barbara smiled shyly and took off the coat that had covered her partial nakedness.

Taya looked again at the woman in front of her with admiration. She then looked up to meet Barbara's eyes. This time, there was no mistaking the intent or the sexual desire in Taya's eyes.

Barbara took a step back and turned around as Taya approached her. Taya stopped mere inches away from the woman who seemed to be trembling from fear, waiting to see what she would do next.

"If I wanted to hurt you I would have already," Taya whispered into her ear. "Come, let's eat. I'm hungry."

Taya walked out of the room as Barbara quickly slipped the long T-shirt on.

†

Barbara followed Taya to the kitchen and was not surprised to find it almost as empty as the rest of the apartment.

Taya stood in front of the microwave waiting for the food that they were to consume to be done. She turned at that instance and was taken aback for a moment at seeing Barbara.

"Can I help with dinner?"

Taya saw that Barbara was trying to keep it together and the strain was beginning to show in the lovely woman's face.

"Not much to do. I don't cook," Taya said, turning to open a drawer. "You could put these on the table." She handed Barbara two forks and two knives.

Barbara took them and Taya noticed how she tried to avoid the mere contact of skin.

"Okay."

"I have some wine if you would like some with the pasta."

"Yes, that would be lovely," Barbara said, caught off guard by the sudden smile on the Taya's face. "What?"

"Do you always speak that way?" Taya asked jokingly.

"What way?" Barbara sounded peeved.

"That would be lovely…" Taya snickered.

She stared at the blonde for a moment. The forlorn look on Barbara's face made her feel bad about the fun she had poked at the other woman's expense.

Barbara left the kitchen but before she walked out Taya noticed tears in those beautiful blue eyes.

"Fuck," Taya said under her breath. She walked around the kitchen like a cat and when she was about to go to the other room to…to do what? The microwave signaled that dinner was done.

She brought the whole platter of pasta and placed it between the two plates on the table.

Barbara was standing by the window looking out into the dark street below.

"Why did you bring me here?" she asked softly, still looking out into the night.

Taya turned toward the woman, unsure how to answer such a simple question. Why not tell her the truth? she asked herself. Tell her why you brought her here.

"Are you going to give me back to them when you are done?" Barbara asked softly, still with her back to her.

"No," Taya finally answered. "I won't do that."

Barbara turned toward her and raised her chin defiantly but the whole posture was lost when Taya saw the tears she was trying to control.

"In the morning I will take you home," Taya said softly and put her hand out for Barbara to take. "Come, dinner will get cold."

Barbara hesitated defiantly for a mere minute but the point was made and taken.

Taya took the soft hand in hers. Something inside her regretted the separation when she released it a moment later.

†

They ate in relative silence. Barbara barely touched her food but consumed the wine.

"Eat," Taya said as she lifted the fork to her mouth.

"I'm not very hungry." Barbara remained looking at her food. She had not looked at Taya since sitting down to eat.

"More wine?"

"No, thank you."

Taya smiled at the woman across from her. Even at this time she never forgot her manners. The smile quickly disappeared when Barbara looked up and Taya saw the fear she was trying to control.

"Are you going to hurt me?"

"Do you like pain?" Taya asked her point-blank.

"No," Barbara answered, visibly trying to control her fear.

"No, I won't hurt you," Taya said as she stood up and picked up her plate. She was walking out of the room when she suddenly stopped. With her back to Barbara she spoke. "Don't try running out of the apartment…you won't get very far and this time I might not be able to find you in time."

"What will be the difference?" Barbara said harshly, letting some of her anger express itself.

Taya quickly turned to face her. All the coldness of her eyes was directed sharply at Barbara, who was taken aback by the look.

"You are going to like it and you will be alive in the morning," Taya said with a voice as cold as steel.

Barbara stared at her for a moment. "You are not like them," she said as her voice shook with controlled fear.

An evil smile appeared in Taya's face. "No, I am worse because I know better."

Barbara could find nothing to say to that but shook her head and began to go for the door.

Taya put the plates back on the table and reached the door at the same time Barbara did.

Barbara turned around with her back against the door, and Taya's body pressed against hers. Barbara's eyes filled with unshed tears and her lower lip began to shake.

Taya looked at her mouth and like a spell pulling her she was powerless to stop the beckoning. At first she touched Barbara's lips softly with her own. She could feel them quiver and the thought of that intoxicated her. All the reason she had fought so hard to keep control of disappeared.

Slowly she kissed the soft, warm mouth that she had tried so hard not to look at during dinner. And as before, her senses were filled yet again with the softness of the woman in her arms. Her mouth trailed down Barbara's neck slowly, sucking and biting lightly at the soft skin. Then she buried her face again in the blond woman's hair and she was powerless to stop the moan of pleasure that escaped her mouth.

Her lips brushed Barbara's ear and again sought those lips that had cast their spell on her. This time, when her mouth covered Barbara's she was surprised when her lips opened and she felt the woman in her arms leaning against her.

Taya's hand cupped Barbara's breast and lightly squeezed it as her other hand went behind Barbara's back to pull her closer to her still. Her mouth was in overdrive and it hungered. She pulled away and tore off Barbara's T-shirt, leaving her with breasts totally exposed.

Taya's mouth went down on a nipple, sucking on it hard as her hand went down and cupped Barbara's ass, pulling her against her.

"Ahhhh…" Barbara moaned as her head fell back, reeling with sensations of pleasure she had never known existed.

Impatient that she could not get enough of Barbara fast enough, Taya released her and started pulling her slacks and underwear to the floor.

Barbara was in a daze as she watched Taya remove her clothing, then met Taya's eyes as her mouth was coming up again to ravage her own. Barbara's hands reached for Taya's face and pulled her to her.

Taya captured her lips and pulled her hard against her own body, walking her backward to the bedroom. She fell on top of Barbara on the bed and again began to kiss and bite and suck on the beautiful body beneath her.

Barbara, who had never experienced such pleasure, wantonly begged Taya not to stop.

Taya's mouth kissed down over her abdomen and Barbara's intake of breath was the only sign of surprise as Taya began to suck her hard between her legs. Barbara's head rolled from side to side as wave after wave of orgasms filled her body. When she cried out in pleasure Taya's fingers thrust inside her, bringing her even higher than she had ever imagined possible.

✝

Barbara lay in blissful state of ecstasy. As her eyes focused she felt her dark-haired partner lie on top of her and kiss her mouth ardently. Her eyes opened and were met by those dark eyes that had earlier filled her with dread.

"I want to make you mine," Taya said passionately.

"Yes," Barbara said and nodded as she kissed those lips above her again.

She was surprised when Taya got up and removed all her clothes and stood in front of Barbara in all her glory. Barbara took in the whole woman. Her thighs were strong and her body was chiseled. Her eyes traveled to full breasts whose nipples were hard and begging to be sucked. Barbara's mouth opened in anticipation. Her own hunger surprised her as her eyes sought Taya's.

Taya pulled open the drawer on the nightstand, never releasing Barbara's eyes from her own. She pulled out a harness with a large dildo attached to it. Barbara stared at it then at Taya.

Taya strapped on the harness and as she tightened it Barbara's breathing became strained. Taya could see in her eyes that her passion was being replaced by fear. Taya quickly spread Barbara's legs and got on top of her but did not enter her. She hovered over Barbara and waited.

"No rush…I want to look at you, my beautiful lover," Taya said in a voice filled with passion. "I want to go inside you slowly and take my time. I won't rush you." Her mouth began to tease one of Barbara's nipples by licking it hard with her tongue. Slowly she began to feel Barbara's body respond to her caresses.

"I won't fuck you until you ask me," Taya said to reassure the woman beneath her. "And you are going to ask me, *querida mía*." Taya growled as she began to suck on Barbara's hard nipple, her other hand squeezing the other nipple unmercifully.

"Taya, oh God! Taya!" Barbara moaned unable to stand the onslaught of pleasure. Her hips rose, begging for the pleasure that penetration would provide. Barbara could not hold off any longer. "Fuck me. Please fuck me," Barbara begged.

Taya filled her in one powerful thrust. "Ahhhh…" Taya thought she would come in that one moment. Never had she experienced such pleasure in this degree with any other woman. She felt Barbara's legs come up around her and both bodies began to ride the pumping action with harder and harder thrusts.

"Come with me…oh God, come with me, I can't hold it anymore," Taya growled in desperation.

"Yes, Taya…fuck me. Please fuck me," Barbara begged. Her words became moans of pleasure that she could no longer control.

"Ahhhhhhhh…" Both women yelled in unison.

†

Shots rang out during the night and Barbara woke up with a start. She looked around the dark room. She could hear more shots not too far away and loud voices.

An arm wrapped itself around her abdomen and pulled her back against a warm, hard body. "Come, *querida*, nothing will hurt you."

Taya pulled her closer to her and she felt completely protected from the horrors of the night. She felt a light kiss on her ear. "Sleep, *querida*. I won't let anything hurt you."

Barbara smiled as her eyes closed and pulled the arms around her closer to her and sleep was once again welcomed.

Chapter Two

The light of day brought to life the reality of what had occurred during the night. Barbara opened her eyes slowly and realized she was unable to move. She was partially covered by Taya, who was sleeping on top of her.

She tried to slide out slowly and became very still as Taya began to stir. A few moments went by and once again she felt Taya's breathing stabilize. Barbara tried to slide from under Taya, again to no avail. She turned her head and came face-to-face with those dark eyes that looked straight at her.

Barbara stopped breathing and could not find the words to utter.

"Good morning," Taya said as she lifted herself on her elbow above Barbara.

"Good morning," Barbara said as a blush spread across her face.

"I want breakfast," Taya said seductively.

"Breakfast is…do you have coffee?" Barbara was confused by what was being said.

"Querida, I want to eat what your body will give me," Taya said huskily as her eyes mirrored the passion of her words.

"No…" Barbara protested, but her body was already betraying her as she felt herself get wet with anticipation.

Taya went down between Barbara's legs and began to feed.

When it was all over and Taya was sated Barbara surprised her by seeking her mouth.

Taya was tempted to push her away for only a moment. She had been the one to take and to give pleasure always. She had never allowed anyone to touch her. Yet, this woman—who had somehow gone from prisoner to...to?—was asking to touch her. She hesitated for only a moment and then surrendered to her desire to be touched. Barbara began shyly and as Taya's responses began to grow she allowed herself to follow her own wants.

Barbara surprised Taya by slowly kissing and caressing toward her groin. When Barbara was between her legs and was about to taste Taya, the woman looked up suddenly. For a brief moment Barbara saw the hidden vulnerability. With a soft smile on her lips that went all the way to her eyes she lowered her mouth to feed.

Taya thought she would come in that very moment when she first began to suck. No one had ever taken her this way. She had never given herself to anyone to be pleasured like this before. She brought her hips up higher, wanting to feel Barbara's mouth closer to her sex. Barbara pulled her hips closer to her still and began to tease her with her tongue in a hard and methodical manner.

Taya thought she would go mad as her hips began to buck as orgasm upon orgasm racked her body. "Barbara...oh God! Barbara, don't stop! Please don't stop!"

✝

Barbara got out of the shower and put on the clean T-shirt and blue jeans that Taya had given her. Her clothes from the day before were unsalvageable. Taya's clothes were a little big on her but under the circumstances, not a bad fit she told herself. Barbara let out a nervous giggle.

She looked at herself in the mirror and wondered what now. Never in her life had she thought that what had occurred in the last twenty-four hours would ever happen to her. If she were honest with herself she did not regret what she had felt and done with Taya.

Taya was in the kitchen having taken her shower earlier. She was dressed as usual all in black with black cowboy boots, which added another inch or so to her already tall height of five nine. Opening cupboards she realized there was nothing to offer Barbara for breakfast. She had teabags. She could always offer her tea, she thought.

"Hi." She heard a voice from behind her and smiled before turning around.

"Hi," Taya said, leaning against the sink behind her. "Want some tea?"

Barbara gave her a quirky smile. "You're a tea drinker?"

"No, I…I can't even make a decent cup of coffee." Taya laughed as she ran her fingers through her dark hair.

"Well, if you have the coffee, I can make it." Barbara laughed and opened the cupboard closest to her before Taya's hand reached out to stop her.

Taya grabbed her hand too late. The cupboard that Barbara opened was empty but for two handguns. Suddenly the reality of who Taya was and how she had gotten here became too real to ignore or sugarcoat.

The light banter between them was gone. Barbara looked from the guns, to Taya's face, to her hand still in Taya's iron grip.

Taya released her and closed the cupboard without looking at Barbara.

"Sorry, I have no coffee," was all she said as she walked to the refrigerator and took out two diet Cokes and offered one to Barbara.

Barbara took it silently.

The silence that grew between them began to smother Taya. What did it matter what this woman thought? She had gotten what she wanted from her. She had wanted to fuck her and she had. What did she expect…a repeat performance? Taya shook her head trying to dislodge the thought that she knew had already embedded itself in her brain. Yes, I want to see her again…no, I want to fuck her again no more and no less.

Taya turned away from Barbara, arguing with her own demons. She is no different than the rest…I liked fucking her…I want to do it again a few more times before I move on, that's all!

When she had convinced herself that was all she wanted out of the woman, Taya turned around to face Barbara.

"Are you going to take me home now?" Barbara asked as she looked up to meet Taya's eyes.

"As promised," Taya said with a smile, trying to lighten the discomfort between them. "Come here," Taya beckoned. She did not wait and met Barbara halfway.

She took Barbara in her arms and again felt all her senses come to life as she had from the very first moment. Why always this reaction? Taya asked herself yet again.

"You are so soft, *querida*," Taya said out loud as she leaned down and tenderly kissed Barbara's lips. All that mattered to her at that moment was that Barbara was in her arms and her lips were soft and welcoming.

✝

Taya came back from the other room wearing her long black leather coat. She was carrying Barbara's coat and handed it to her. She put on her sunglasses and turned toward Barbara.

"Ready?"

"Yes."

They both went down the stairs then out a back door. A few feet away Taya unlocked the door of a large garage, without visible windows that Barbara could see.

Barbara's eyes got as big as two saucers when she saw Taya get on a huge black and chromed Harley Davidson.

Taya put a boot on the pedal and with one good kick the huge machine growled as it came to life.

"Hop on," Taya said as she handed Barbara a helmet.

Barbara just stared at her.

Taya smiled then pulled her to her and kissed her hard on the mouth. She pulled away and took the helmet from Barbara's hands, helping her put it on.

When Barbara climbed on behind her she pulled her closer to her and made sure she understood she had to hang on tight.

The black iron animal, as Barbara thought of the bike, pulled out and they began to fly through the dilapidated streets and past boarded up houses. It all seemed unreal somehow…and as she looked around she suddenly realized that she was lucky to be alive…and…Taya… What could she make of Taya?

Within minutes they were out onto Broadway, Newark's once prominent street, and then out of the city toward Upper Montclair. The city became familiar to Barbara and people walked the street totally oblivious of the menacing shadows that hovered so close by. Barbara closed her eyes and held Taya tighter.

Taya noticed the change and placed one hand on top of Barbara's for a moment in reassurance. Why did it matter, she asked herself, staring straight ahead. The sooner she could drop off this woman the better she told herself. Out of the pens and out of my world, thought Taya to herself as she crossed an invisible line that few knew existed.

After about thirty minutes Barbara looked around again. They were a few blocks from her home.

Taya pulled into her street and the bike slowed down until it came to a complete stop when they pulled into her driveway.

They sat for a moment without moving, both deep in their own thoughts.

Taya turned off the bike and Barbara removed her arms from around her.

Barbara got off the bike and removed her helmet, running her fingers through her hair.

Taya looked at the house. "Big," was all she said.

"Yes." Barbara handed her the helmet.

Both women were unable, for some reason, to break the tie that bound them.

"How did you know where I lived?" Barbara suddenly asked.

"How would someone like me know anything?" Taya replied without humor in her voice.

Barbara waited and Taya looked away.

"Why are you living there?" Barbara asked softly. She was surprised that Taya still did not react.

"What does it matter?" Barbara heard Taya answer softly, still looking away.

"It's not you somehow."

Taya turned quickly toward her. "You think you know me because I fucked you?"

Barbara was taken aback by the sudden attack.

"Go back to your big house and your mink coat and get fucked...oh but wait!" Taya was being particularly crude when she added, "By what I could tell you have never been really fucked well, have you?"

Barbara was stunned and about to run into the house when Taya's iron grip pulled her face a breath away from her own. "Maybe if you are a good girl I'll come back and fuck you up the ass next time."

Barbara pulled away in horror and ran toward the house. Taya pulled out of the driveway and flew down the street as fast as her bike would take her. Both were running in their own way.

Barbara slammed her front door shut, locked it, and leaned against it. Tears ran down her face as she began to sob and slide down to the floor.

Taya told herself over and over again that Barbara had been nothing but a good fuck.

✝

Uncontrollable anger seeped into every breath and every action of Taya's body. She flew back to the pens. Heads turned as they saw the Black Angel of Death fly by. The shadows receded, not wanting to meet their maker that day. They knew she had justice to dish out, and the end was never good.

Taya pulled up in front of a decaying warehouse. There were a few men outside. She got off her bike and walked past them. They nodded in her direction out of respect as she passed them. One crossed himself as she walked by.

Her bike had been left unattended yet all the men outside knew that she had seen them and it was their responsibility to protect it with their lives if necessary. They knew that death was more desirable then receiving punishment from Black Angel.

A few had tested her patience and had not lived to tell. Her beauty surprised and disarmed most men and women. Her capacity to inflict pain was such that one would gladly pray for death rather than survival. That was an unquestionable truth. Taya was the Boss. She was the Black

Angel of the pens. None of the dealers, the bookies, the whores and even some cops questioned her authority. They paid her tribute in percentages of their take. She had a brilliant mind and an iron will, and she knew how to reward loyalty. No one crossed her and lived long. Only those too stupid ever tried.

Everyone in the pens had heard about Jake's stupidity the day before. No one wanted to be in his shoes today.

When the door of the warehouse banged open everyone inside froze. Those that were cutting the coke and bagging it continued their work but kept one eye on Taya. All the rest scurried away. The brave souls that remained stared as she walked in. She looked around and smiled the smile that made them all shake with fear.

Taya's eyes found Stanley standing close to Jake. Her steps echoed as her boot heels connected with the cement floor.

She stopped about twenty feet away and with a crook of her index finger called Jake over. He knew he was in trouble and, as he hobbled over to where Taya stood, he began to babble.

"Taya…I was high yesterday. It won't ever happen again. You have first cut of everything, Taya. These are your pens," Jake managed to get out as he stood in front of her.

She still wore her sunglasses so he couldn't see her eyes, which made him break into a sweat.

"Leg hurt?" Taya asked softly. "I would hate to think I hurt you."

"No, it's okay," Jake said in relief.

Suddenly his face became distorted with pain. He looked down and saw her knife sticking out of his leg, her hand still wrapped around its handle. He looked up at her in shock, unable to utter a word and afraid to.

"Leg hurt?" She asked him again even softer than before. All around them took a step back in terror.

Jake had a horrified grimace on his face as he shook his head. A smile spread across her face.

"You seemed to think I didn't have a right to a piece of ass yesterday, Jake," she said menacingly. "When you know that what you have is what I allow you to have." Taya was finding it hard to control the anger building inside her.

Weakness in the pens meant death. And she was not weak.

"That particular piece of ass is mine, Jake." She looked around as she gave the knife a twist.

All nodded in understanding. She turned back to Jake again.

"You wanted to fuck my woman, Jake." Taya spat at him.

"Taya, I didn't know she was yours, I swear!" Jake began to plead with her. "I swear, Taya, I swear." He was crying by this time.

Jake had been a problem for a while now. But this time he had challenged her authority. This time he had gone too far.

She took the knife out of his leg and he moaned but remained standing. He didn't dare move.

She looked around at the others. "I could understand you wanting to fuck her…she is such a good fuck." Taya smiled sardonically.

Jake smiled in agreement, the smile a mistake that he would never understand. Because no matter how many times Taya told herself she didn't care about this woman, she could still smell her and taste her. She moaned at the thought then shook her head to dislodge the vision that was quickly filling her mind.

Taya got serious again as she turned to him. "I could understand you wanting to fuck her, Jake. But you touched my woman. You put your filthy hands on my property, Jake."

Jake began to whimper in fear, shaking his head as he stared into the dark lenses of her sunglasses.

"Was my woman soft, Jake?" Taya asked.

"No," Jake blurted out in fear.

"No?" Taya spat out.

"No, Taya, no!"

"Are you saying I have bad taste, Jake?" She was playing with him like a cat with a mouse.

"No, Taya, she is the best piece of ass I've ever seen. She's soft too, Taya. Very soft," Jake blurted out.

She took out her Glock and shot him in the head without hesitation. She leaned over to Stanley, took the scarf from around his neck and wiped the blood and brain matter that had landed on her coat as if it had been a little dirt that she was removing. Jake lay on the ground.

"No one touches what's mine," Taya said loud enough for all to hear. She then turned to Stanley. He was barely breathing.

"You didn't know she was mine, did you, Stanley?"

"No, Taya. No," he said nervously.

"Yes, you backed off right away, I remember. You know what she looks like now, don't you, Stanley. You are going to make sure they all know, aren't you?"

Stanley nodded and remained silent.

She looked around and directed her comment to the general audience. "Everything in the pens is mine unless I give it to you." No one contradicted her. She was the leader and not obeying meant a painful and agonizing death.

Taya looked at Stanley again. "Stanley, the south pen is all yours now, for knowing when to listen and for your respect of my property. And for your loyalty, Stanley." Taya then smiled.

"Thank you, Taya." Stanley was more than satisfied. Jake was forgotten. He had gone up in the ranks.

"And if you ever see my woman again…"

"I will have men all over the pens to make sure that she is not touched in any way, Taya," Stanley said quickly and she smiled. He knew she was satisfied and that meant his involvement in yesterday's event was forgotten.

"Clean this up, Stanley."

"Consider it done, Taya."

"Good."

Chapter Three

Barbara wasn't sure how long she had cried while sitting on the floor. She got up slowly; her body felt sore. The weight of the world seemed to be on top of her. Gradually she walked up the staircase. The world as she knew it had changed colors and nothing would ever be the same again.

She walked into her bedroom and looked around, took in all the details. Everything matched, and that struck her for some reason. Her life was full of things that matched. All with so-called good taste, artfully chosen to impress…impress whom? And yet if she were honest with herself it had never looked emptier. At least Taya was honest. Taya… Even thinking of her name made her hurt.

She took off her clothes and let them drop to the floor as she walked. She wanted a shower; she felt unclean somehow. In the view of daylight Taya had made it all very clear, and it all made her feel dirty somehow. She had, in Taya's own words, just been someone to fuck.

Barbara turned on the shower and stepped in. She let the water wash over her body and as it did she began to cry all over again.

✝

It was eight p.m. when Taya once again entered the warehouse. Stanley looked up in surprise and proceeded to walk toward her.

"The shipment is almost ready for distribution," he assured her immediately. Now as head of the south pens he was in charge of the distribution of coke. Not only had his rank more than tripled, but within twenty-four hours his power had grown as well. He knew he had to prove himself to Black Angel. She had raised him from the gutter to the top. He was not about to fail.

"Good, I want it on the street by tonight." She looked at him, waiting for him to challenge her.

He knew immediately it was a test and failure was not an option. "We should be out of here by ten, then the cleaners can come in. I'll see to it, Taya."

Taya looked at him in deep speculation. Perhaps Stanley had been the one she had been looking for. Only time would tell.

"Keep it smooth, Stanley. Make sure you pick up cash or don't deliver."

He nodded.

"All else taken care of?"

"Dust to dust," was all he said.

"Good. Later." She walked out.

When he saw her leave the building Stanley finally took a deep breath and his body began to relax again.

Taya got on her bike. She began the nightly ride around her jungle. This was her world and the pens were hers. The sides of her mouth turned up. Dust to dust. She laughed lightly, remembering what Stanley had said. Nice line, I'll have to remember it, she thought. In other words, Jake's body had been cremated. Nothing was left to tie her or implicate her to him. It was one of the rules of her world, of the pens. They all lived and survived by certain laws. And the law had been enforced.

†

Barbara sat on the sofa, her legs tucked under her, staring straight ahead into nothing. She never noticed as the light of the day gradually disappeared and the shadows of night quietly arrived.

"Barbara? Barbara?" She seemed to hear from a distance.

She turned slowly and shook her head as she stared at her sister, Dale, who was standing in front of her.

"Barbara," Dale said softly as she knelt down to look into Barbara's face. "You okay, sweetheart?"

Barbara stared at her sister, then suddenly all the turmoil inside her came forth and she threw herself into her sister's arms.

Both women sank to the floor. Dale wasn't sure what had happened but it had to be more than she had counted on. She held Barbara tightly, trying to console her.

"It's okay, Barb. It's going to be okay. I've been calling you since last night. Mom is worried sick, what happened, sweetie? Where have you been?" Dale asked gently.

Barbara pulled away from her sister's protective embrace. She sat, mirroring her sister, with her back against the sofa and wiped her face.

"Barbara, where have you been?" Dale asked again.

"I…" Her hand shakily went up to her neck.

Dale noticed and looked at her sister, even more worried than before.

"What did he do, Barb? So help me I'm going to kill that son of a bitch!"

Barbara looked at her sister. "No…I mean…" How could she tell Dale anything when she wasn't sure herself of anything?

"Sorry," Dale said softly. "Slowly…take your time," she added as she waited patiently for her sister to speak.

"I went to the lawyer's yesterday…God, yesterday seems so far away," Barbara said as she stared in front of her again. She shook her head and began to speak again. "Jeff finally agreed that I would get custody of the boys. He is giving them a hard time on financial disclosures, but they expected that."

"Sounds like all is progressing well then. You have the boys," Dale said happily. "I know how much that worried you."

Barbara then turned toward her sister and smiled. "Yes."

"What is he not disclosing?"

"Oh…some accounts that came up. They have to do with investments, that sort of thing. Apparently he has been investing for some time now. He has bought real estate, among other things, without my knowledge to the point of six million dollars."

"Hmmmm…"

"I got out of the lawyer's office with the realization that I had been living with a stranger." Barbara looked at Dale with pained eyes. "Years…years before I ever realized that we had problems he was doing all this. I was living, sleeping, and making love to a stranger, Dale. I didn't know him at all! That really scared me," she finished as tears began to roll down her face again.

"It kind of opened up the wounds all over again, huh?"

"In a way…yes. How could I have been so blind to it all?" Barbara wiped the tears away. "It's like…I had been walking, talking, and living in a dream for years and none of it was real. My whole marriage was a lie. He wants to settle as soon as possible. Apparently Joanna is pregnant."

"I'm sorry, Barbara," Dale said sadly.

Joanna, they had found out a mere six months ago, was Jeff's mistress of three years. Barbara had gone to meet some friends for lunch when they saw Joanna and Jeff coming out of a hotel, kissing goodbye passionately in plain daylight.

Barbara had been devastated. But no longer blinded by trust she began to ask questions and what followed was a nightmare that became quickly too real.

Dale had received her sister's anguished call when it all happened. She knew that Barbara was strong but the effect of so much betrayal had shaken her to the core. And the boys had gone from acting out to sullen quietness. At least Jeff had agreed to custody. That, at least, her sister would not have to worry about.

"Then…" Barbara looked away from her sister. "Then...something happened."

"What?" Dale asked softly. Dear God, what more will she have to deal with? Dale thought to herself as she held her sister's hand tightly in support.

"I…" Barbara looked at Dale then down at their hands clasped together, "I was attacked…two men tried to…"

"Oh, my God, Barbara!" Dale feared the worst.

Barbara looked up quickly. "No, I'm okay."

"How? Where?"

"I wasn't paying attention where I was going. My mind was so confused and I walked into a place I should never have been." Barbara tried to explain quickly so as not to worry Dale more than she was already.

Dale had always been there. She was the older sister and as such Barbara had always confided and counted on her. But this? How could she talk to Dale about this?

"Are you sure you're okay?" Dale asked, still very concerned.

"Yes…no, I was so scared, Dale." Barbara looked at her sister. "I thought they were going to…if..." Barbara trailed off. She ran shaky fingers through her hair. "I was saved by a dark stranger…who in turn showed me yet again what an easy mark I must be." She laughed with a nervous giggle.

"Barbara…I don't understand."

"I don't understand myself," Barbara said barely above a whisper.

"Barb? Were you raped last night?" Dale asked gently as she placed her hand on top of her sister's shaking one.

Barbara looked up and met her sister's gaze and as she did her eyes filled with tears.

"Raped? No…" Barbara said softly and looked away. "I wasn't raped."

Dale was confused and yet she sensed that something was still not right.

"Dale...I…" Barbara said as she looked at her sister again and began to cry.

"Why didn't you come home last night?" Dale asked gently as she held on to her sister's hands.

"I couldn't…at first I couldn't leave and then I didn't want to. We made love all night long, Dale," Barbara finally blurted out.

Dale's eyes got bigger and bigger.

"I was terrified, excited, and never more satisfied. I'm so scared, Dale. I'm so scared." Barbara collapsed into her sister's arms again. "I feel like my whole life is spinning out of my control and I can't stop it."

Dale hung on to her and held back the questions that she knew Barbara could not answer right now.

"I'm so scared, Dale. I'm so scared."

✝

Taya walked into her apartment and locked the door behind her. She looked around and felt the emptiness and the lack of things, which usually gave her such satisfaction, close in around her. She went to her bedroom and began taking her clothes off. She still felt Barbara on her skin. That must be remedied. She would just wash her off.

She went into the bathroom to take a shower. First though, she needed something for her horrible headache. Turning toward the medicine cabinet over the sink she noticed the earrings next to the sink. Taya picked them up slowly and held them in her palm. Barbara, she thought to herself. The mere thought of the woman's name seemed to take a firm hold on some part of her.

Taya's eyes closed as she remembered their owner. She could feel Barbara's hands on her body even now. The feel of Barbara's mouth was still fresh and the taste of her was still in Taya's mouth. She opened her eyes slowly and stared at her reflection in the mirror. *Why did I let her touch me?* My mother would say it's Santería. Taya pushed all thoughts such as that one immediately out of her mind. How had that happened?

"What do I do now?" she asked the reflection staring back at her.

Chapter Four

Dale and Barbara never did discuss what had happened to Barbara that night. Barbara just closed up. Dale tried to bring it up several times until Barbara finally told her it had been something that happened and she wanted to just forget about it. She thought, in view of the circumstances, it was probably best left that way. Barbara would talk to her when she was ready.

Within two weeks Barbara began to feel comfortable in her daily routine again. It occurred to her, as she dropped off her boys, Sean and Eric, for soccer practice, that she liked the reliability of just doing. As she began to analyze that, something more frightening occurred to her: if you just went through the motions, you just did but you didn't necessarily feel. Had she been just going through the motions? Not looking, not seeing, not feeling with Jeff? Was that what had hit her so hard? Had she just not wanted to question?

Barbara shook her head. "Enough," she said aloud and pulled out of the school parking lot. No matter how many times she went through it all in her head nothing made any sense. Sometimes, that was the way it was and it was best just to keep going.

The next day, Barbara's controlled resolve and belief that she was once again comfortable in her routine was shaken to its core. She and Dale were taking the boys to a new place in town that served up pizza and games for children.

"Will you guys keep it down back there," Dale said to the boys in the backseat as she tried to speak to Barbara, who sat beside her in the front seat of her Explorer. "A friend in the office told me about this place," she was saying to Barbara.

"We better get there soon. I think the natives are restless," Barbara said as she looked at the boys sitting in the back.

"Mom, I'm starving. When are we gonna get there?" Brian, Dale's nine-year-old son whined.

"Soon."

Suddenly, out of nowhere, a black motorcycle pulled up next to them. Barbara felt her body react, as the sound seemed to fill her. She began to shake and her breath came irregularly. She turned toward the window and felt her world spin as she stared at the black-clad rider with a black helmet on. She raised a shaky hand to her pale face.

"Barbara? Barbara? Are you all right?" Dale asked with concern obvious in her voice. "Barbara?"

Barbara felt herself floating in limbo, totally oblivious to the concern she was causing.

Dale pulled out of traffic and onto the shoulder. She turned to face her sister. The boys in the back became very quiet.

"Barbara? Sweetheart, are you okay?"

"Mom?"

"It's okay, guys. Mom is just tired. Let's just give her a minute," Dale tried to reassure the boys in the backseat.

Barbara stared at her sister. Her shaking began to subside and her eyes began to focus. She nodded. "Yes, I'm sorry. I just got a little dizzy."

When the sound of a motorcycle was heard in the distance again, Barbara flinched.

Barbara could tell Dale was beginning to get really worried. But she needed to think this through on her own before she could discuss what had happened between her and Taya with anyone.

✝

It had been a week since the incident in the car with Dale and Barbara had convinced herself that she was in control of her life again. It had all been just an aberration. It had been the stress she was under. It had been…whatever it had been it was over.

Barbara got home and went straight for the kitchen. Today was soccer night so dinner was always a light fare. She and Dale alternated dropping off and picking up the boys for every practice and game, and whoever dropped off served dinner.

The phone rang and Barbara grabbed the hot dog buns out of the breadbox as she answered.

"Hello… Hi, Jean…sure, I've got some eggs you can have…come on over. I'm in the kitchen so just come on in, the door will be open." Barbara hung up the phone and went to unlock the front door for her friend, who lived two houses down.

Barbara went back to the kitchen and turned on the radio. An old favorite came on and she started singing along with Tony Orlando and Dawn as she pulled the hot dogs out of the refrigerator along with the potato and macaroni salad she had bought earlier.

"La..la…la la la… 'Hey girl whatcha doin' down there…'"

She was surprised to hear the doorbell. "Come on in. It's open," she yelled and went to pull out a bowl of layered Jell-O to surprise the boys. She began to sing again.

"'You don't even know me I love you… Oh my darlin', Knock three times on the ceiling if you want me… Twice on the pipe means you ain't gonna show…'"

She was still singing when she turned around with a friendly smile for her friend, Jean. Suddenly she felt like someone had pulled the floor out from under her.

In front of her stood Taya, in all her fine black garb, including sunglasses, smiling. The bowl that Barbara was holding slipped out of her hands and crashed loudly on the floor. Barbara, however, did not move a muscle.

"You sing nice." Taya's velvety voice reached out to her.

Taya knelt down at the same time Barbara did to pick up the broken pieces of glass from the shattered bowl.

"Let me help you," Taya said softly.

Barbara was still unable to utter a sound.

The broken glass pieces were picked up in silence, then Barbara pulled out some kitchen towels to pick up the Jell-O.

Neither had uttered another word. Cleanup completed both women once again stood facing one another. Barbara took a few steps back as the love song on the radio continued.

Taya smiled seductively. Barbara turned off the radio.

"I'm sorry I frightened you. I rang and you yelled to come in," Taya said gently.

"I'm expecting a friend."

"I see. I always did have bad timing," Taya said and tried smiling. She was sorry to see that Barbara was obviously not happy to see her.

Both again waited for the other to speak.

"I came…" Taya began to say when someone came in behind her.

"Hi, Barbara."

"Jean, hello."

Jean looked from Barbara to Taya.

"Jean, this is…"

"Taya, nice to meet you." Taya smiled and held her hand out to Jean who took it with a smile of her own.

"Is that your bike outside?" Jean asked enthusiastically.

"Yes."

"It's really beautiful. My husband and I are always reminiscing about how romantic it is to ride into the sunset on a bike like that. You know…rebel without a cause and all that," Jean added as she swooned.

Taya smiled politely.

"Hey, Barb? Earth to Barbara…you there?" Jean said to her friend who seemed to be in some type of trance.

"I'm sorry, Jean. It's been a long day. Eggs right?" Barbara turned toward the refrigerator once more and pulled out a carton of eggs and handed them over to her friend.

"Thanks, I only need six."

"That's okay. Take them, I've got another carton."

"Okay, thanks Barb. I gotta run." Jean then turned to Taya. "It was nice meeting you, Taya."

"Likewise."

When the front door closed Barbara immediately went on the defensive. "What are you doing here?"

Taya raised an eyebrow. No one spoke to her like that! "I told you I would come back."

"No!" Barbara scooted behind the island in her kitchen.

"You haven't forgotten me already have you, querida?" Taya said coyly as she stepped closer to the island. "And here I was thinking that you would be welcoming me back nice and proper like."

"Taya, please go. I want you to go," Barbara said with a plea.

Taya stopped and stared at Barbara for a moment. "Do you?" Taya asked softly. "Do you want me to go, *querida mía*?" For a moment Barbara thought that she heard sadness in the woman's voice and saw it reflected in those dark eyes.

Barbara hesitated and that was all the encouragement that Taya needed. She quickly went around the island and caught Barbara between the sink and herself as she tried to escape.

Both women heard the other's breath grow heavy as physical contact was made. Both sets of eyes focused on the other's mouth.

"Did you miss me, *querida*?" Taya asked huskily, still only looking at Barbara's lips. Taya leaned into Barbara's body.

Barbara was about to speak when Taya closed the distance between them. When Taya's mouth connected with Barbara's she thought she finally understood the meaning of bliss. Her mouth begged and pleaded. Not until that moment of union did Taya truly understand how much she had needed to taste those lips again.

The passion that had seemed to consume them once before began to intoxicate them again. Taya wasn't sure if the moans of pleasure were coming out of her mouth or Barbara's. All she knew was that Barbara was kissing her back. Barbara's hands were touching her, pulling at her clothes, exciting her breasts and at that moment all reason was lost. All that both women understood and craved was for the hunger to touch, taste, and connect to be fed.

Somehow they made it up to the bedroom. And again, after the urgency passed and the need was filled they only had each other and the reality of a now. Barbara sat up waiting for Taya to say something, and Taya prayed for the right words to come.

"We better get up. My sister will be here soon with her son and mine."

Taya stopped breathing. "You have a son?"

"I have two." Barbara still had her back to her.

"I didn't plan this, Barbara. I didn't come back to haunt you or anything." Taya suddenly wanted to reassure her.

"Then if not for this, why did you come back?" Barbara turned toward her, challenging what she had just heard.

"You left your earrings behind, *querida*," Taya said softly. "I wanted to return them."

Barbara stared at her, not knowing whether she liked the reason or not.

"I can't say I'm sorry I came. As a matter of fact…I came many times, querida," she said without any shame. Taya was uncomfortable with the seriousness of the conversation so she opted for sarcasm.

Barbara flinched at the comment and Taya immediately regretted making it.

"I didn't mean it like that," Taya said softly, looking at Barbara seriously now.

"What did you mean then?" Barbara asked. The answer had become very important all of a sudden. Then the real question she wanted to ask came forth softly. "Why did you really come?"

"I…I wanted…I needed to see you," Taya said and stared at Barbara. Her hand reached out and caressed the face that had been haunting her both day and night. "Are you sorry I came?" Taya's eyes seemed fathomless.

Barbara saw something in those eyes that she perhaps did not want to see. She knew that Taya had told her the truth. She also knew that this could not possibly go anywhere. Barbara shook her head and started to get up. As she did she found her hand in an iron grip.

"You liked it and you know it!" Taya's eyes were cold as steel now.

"Let go of me!"

"Come back here. Your memory needs reminding." Taya pulled her hard and Barbara fell onto the bed again. Taya was on top of her before Barbara realized what was happening.

"Taya, my boys will be home soon. Please let me go," Barbara said nervously.

"Tell me, *querida*, did you miss me?" Taya taunted her.

"Let me up!"

"Shall I show you another spot or two that can give you pleasure?"

"Taya, please!" Barbara gasped for breath. "Please…"

Taya pulled Barbara's arms up over her head and held them there with one hand. The other was between Barbara's legs.

"Oh…querida. You are already wet for me," Taya said as she started rubbing the spot she knew drove Barbara crazy.

"Taya…I didn't want to miss you, but I did," Barbara said between ecstasy and tears. "Please, oh God, Taya, please."

After she made Barbara cry out with pleasure Taya wasn't sure if she wanted her question answered after all. She was filled with a desire to hold onto and caress the body of her lover, something that, up to that point in her life, she had never desired before.

Barbara looked up into the darkness of Taya's eyes and in that moment took Taya's breath away. Taya was about to say something when the phone on the nightstand began to ring. Barbara turned away to pick it up.

"Hello…Dale, yes, pick it up…how long will it take you to get here? … Okay, bye." Barbara hung up the phone and turned toward Taya.

"Dale? Is that him?" Taya asked as she sat on the bed with her back to Barbara.

"Dale is my sister."

"Is there a him?" Taya asked and Barbara could see her back muscles tense.

"There was."

"And now?"

"Now? I am going through a divorce," Barbara said wearily.

Taya turned toward Barbara, searching her face. "Did you love him?"

Barbara looked away for a moment then back at her again. "Once, I thought I did."

"Have there been others?" Taya asked finally the question that really interested her.

"Others?" Barbara wasn't sure what she was asking. "A little late to be concerned about safe sex now, wouldn't you say?" She was angry all of a sudden.

"I practice safe sex," Taya said defensively and realized this was not what she had intended to talk about originally.

Barbara turned toward her, challenging that statement.

"With you, I...I didn't think," Taya said, seeming nervous and uncomfortable.

Barbara saw the apparently secure woman falter and smiled. "I don't sleep around. You don't have to worry."

"I wasn't worried...I..." Taya again seemed uncomfortable.

"I married Jeff when I turned twenty. He was the first. I haven't been with anyone else," Barbara said. Taya looked at her speculatively. "I was tested a few months ago when we split up. After all, he, I found out, had slept with everyone and their mother too." Barbara could not control the anger of that last statement. "So, you don't need to worry. I, on the other hand..."

Taya walked over to her. "I practice safe sex, Barbara. I do the fucking okay! No one enters me and I don't suck anyone. It's all quite safe I assure you."

"And me?" Barbara said, challenging her now.

"Yes, I fucked you and I sucked you, and I also let you suck me. But you were the exception," Taya said, daring her to address it.

"Is that supposed to make me feel better?" Barbara said flippantly as she started dressing. She didn't want to know all this. She didn't want to know what Taya did to other women. "I don't want to talk about this, okay."

"I will get tested if it will make you feel better," Taya said as she stood in the same place, still completely naked.

"Oh, dear God!" Barbara said as the enormity of what she had done suddenly hit her.

"Barbara, I don't think that I'm..."

"You don't think? No, you don't think!" Barbara threw back at her.

"Fuck you!" Taya walked away and started putting her clothes on.

Barbara heard a car pulling up in her driveway. She walked over to the window and ran her fingers through her hair. *What now? Oh, my God, what now?*

Barbara looked toward Taya who had her back to her as she dressed. "I'm going down. They're here."

"Fine."

Barbara was opening the bedroom door when Taya came up from behind and pulled her against her. "I will go and get tested tomorrow." she said softly into Barbara's hair. "You don't need to worry," Taya whispered into her ear and kissed it.

Barbara pulled away and went down the staircase without uttering a word.

Taya stood as if she was made of stone. She felt as if Barbara had slapped her.

Fuck this! She grabbed her sunglasses from the nightstand and headed down stairs after looking into the mirror on the vanity and running her fingers through her hair to fix it up a bit.

Chapter Five

Barbara stepped into the kitchen just as Dale and the boys ran in.

"Hi." Barbara said as they all scurried around. "Guys, go wash your hands, okay. Food will be ready in a few."

"Here is the ice cream cake. They begged me. I was weak," Dale said with a smile on her face. "You look refreshed."

"What?" Barbara asked nervously as she ran her fingers through her hair. She took the ice cream cake and placed it inside the refrigerator, avoiding Dale's eyes.

"I just said you looked refreshed," Dale said, confused at how her sister was acting. Something was going on with Barbara, and her patience about not asking her was running to an end.

Barbara turned around and started filling a pot with water to cook the hot dogs. "I took a nap when I got home," Barbara said with her back to Dale.

"Well, you look good. Looks like you needed it."

The pot she had filled with water slipped out of her hands and splashed in the sink. Barbara could see her hands begin to shake. Fortunately Dale can't see me, she told herself. Oh, dear God, just help me get through this.

"Whose bike is outside?"

"Oh…a friend's," Barbara mumbled. "She just dropped by."

Dale was about to ask more questions when a noise caught her attention. She turned in time to see Taya coming down the staircase. The woman she saw was dressed all in black, holding a black leather coat over her shoulder with one finger. Her dark hair seemed windblown. Dale had to admit the woman was beautiful and walked with a sureness that exuded wildness just barely visible under her skin.

The only jewelry she wore were silver earrings that hung from her earlobes and shone in contrast to the all-black attire she wore. With her dark glasses on, Dale had to admit she looked very attractive in a dangerous kind of way. She looked from Taya to Barbara who had turned as well and was also watching Taya's descent down the staircase.

A friend, Barbara had said. Somehow that didn't seem to fit, Dale thought.

Barbara was mesmerized as she stared at the woman who only moments ago had given her body so much pleasure.

God, she is so beautiful, Barbara said to herself.

Dale noticed the exchange of something, though not quite sure what, between the two women, and her curiosity knew no bounds. As she got up her chair slid on the floor, the noise shaking Barbara back to reality.

"Dale, this is the owner of the Harley out front."

"Hi," Dale said as she looked from Taya to Barbara.

"Hello, I'm Taya." Taya walked over slowly to Dale and reached out to shake her hand.

Dale looked toward Barbara who suddenly looked nervous again and had turned toward the sink once more. "Taya was passing by," Barbara said with her back to them both.

As Dale and Taya shook hands Taya looked to where Barbara stood and smiled. She was enjoying seeing the blonde squirm.

"Yes," Taya said as she removed her sunglasses. She smiled seductively then added, "I was just passing by."

"That is some bike," Dale said to change the subject that for some reason was making her uncomfortable.

"Thank you."

"Dinner will be ready in a few minutes," Barbara said as she put the hot dogs on the stove.

"Sounds good," Dale said. "Where did you two meet?" Finally curiosity won out.

Barbara turned to face them both.

"We met..." Barbara and Taya said at the same time. Taya smiled and continued while Barbara froze on the spot. "We met by mutual need."

Barbara thought she was going to faint. Dale looked from her sister to Taya.

"I don't understand." Dale was beginning to get nervous.

"Counseling," Barbara blurted out. "We both attend a women's counseling group."

Taya smiled and said nothing as she looked down at her boots then back up at Barbara.

"I didn't know you were going to counseling," Dale commented, surprised.

"I...yes, I thought it might help," Barbara said, looking toward Taya. She sent a silent plea of help, which to her surprise was answered.

"Sometimes, it helps to share with others. It makes you feel like you are not alone," Taya added with a sincere ring to her voice.

Barbara realized that Taya was playing along.

"Yes, I can understand that. Are you going through a divorce too?" Dale asked Taya sympathetically.

"No, not exactly. It's complicated," Taya added and Dale nodded in understanding.

Taking a step toward Barbara Taya pulled out something from her pocket.

Barbara looked down questioningly.

"Your earrings, querida," Taya said softly.

Barbara seemed to pale a bit as she took them. "Thank you." Barbara looked into Taya's eyes, expressing her gratitude for more than the earrings.

"You're welcome," Taya said softly. She was about to say something else when all three boys ran into the kitchen.

"Mom, Mom! Whose bike is on the driveway?" Eric, her nine-year-old, asked excitedly.

"Mine," Taya said. Suddenly she had the boys' full attention.

"Can I have a ride?" Eric asked excitedly as his brother and cousin stood behind him.

"Sure."

"No!" Barbara said. All eyes turned toward her. Barbara stared at Taya, who raised an eyebrow hiding a mischievous dare.

"Mom, please," Eric objected.

"Mom, come on," Sean pleaded as well.

Barbara looked back at Taya with murder in her eyes.

"How tall are you?" Taya intervened and drew the attention away from Barbara. "A bike is like a weapon. Not only can it hurt you, but if you aren't big enough to control it a bike can kill or hurt someone else."

"I'm big," Eric said immediately.

"Hmmm…" Taya straightened to her full height and stepped in front of him. Eric took a step back as his neck went all the way back to look at her.

"Have you ever hurt anybody with the bike?" Brian asked this time.

Taya looked up at Barbara, questioning. Barbara nodded.

"Yes, I don't ever want that to happen again. What I can do is show you the bike and explain to you how it works. If your mothers think it's okay I can even let you ride behind me in the driveway." Taya looked at Barbara whose eyes looked as if they would bulge out of their sockets.

Uh-oh, bad idea too, Taya told herself after seeing Barbara's reaction again.

"I don't know…" Dale said, looking from Taya to Barbara.

"Dale, why don't you ride with me first," Taya suggested with a smile.

"Come on, Mom, please," Brian begged his mother.

"Oh, no," Dale said, shaking her head. Barbara knew as soon as she did that it was a done deal.

"What do you say, Barbara?" Taya asked her point-blank.

"Please, Mom. Please," Eric and Sean said at the same time.

Barbara was silent, then Taya turned toward Dale. "Come on, you'll love it." Taya grabbed Dale by the arm and the kids followed her outside.

Barbara could not believe it as she followed them too.

†

The boys took to Taya right away. She seemed so out of her element to Barbara and yet the boys had not even thought twice about her at all. Barbara looked on from a safe distance as one by one they rode behind Taya on the Iron Monster as Barbara called it. Taya was like a wild animal in captivity. Somehow Barbara knew that her control was only skin-deep, yet with the boys she was gentle and patiently explained and answered every question they asked. Barbara smiled at that until she remembered where and how she had met Taya. As she remembered she realized that there was no safe ground between two worlds as different as theirs.

"Come guys, dinner. You have school tomorrow too," Barbara called out.

"Oh, Mom," Eric and Sean whined.

"Come on. Let's go," Barbara insisted.

Dale walked up to Taya. "Thanks, it was fun."

"You're welcome. Anytime," Taya said as she helped Eric get off from behind her. She helped him take off his helmet.

The boy looked into her eyes for a moment. Taya was taken aback by the clearness of those innocent eyes.

"When I am big, I'm going to ride a bike like this one," Eric said proudly.

Taya looked down at the boy very seriously. "You will go to school and have another type of life."

Barbara and Dale had heard her and became silent.

"But, Taya, I can do that too," Eric insisted.

Taya tousled his golden hair and smiled sadly. "No, you can't. Go to your mother."

"But you ride a bike, Taya," Sean said as he stood in front of her now too.

"Yes, but you are lucky."

"I don't understand." Eric, as usual, always needed answers.

"What would happen to your mother if you were hurt?" Taya asked the boy seriously.

Eric and Sean looked toward their mother then back at Taya.

"She would cry and be sad," Eric said.

"Do you want that?"

"No," Eric said as she put his head down.

"How about you?" Sean asked her.

"I don't have anyone," Taya said flatly. Eric looked up at her for a while.

Dale looked down and said nothing. Barbara looked away. She didn't want to cultivate feelings for someone she could never understand and whom she was partly terrified of.

"Go now," Taya said to the boys as she turned around and got back on her bike.

What the hell am I doing here anyway? Taya asked herself.

Taya kicked the bike to life and rode away without looking back. She wanted to put as much distance between her and Barbara as she could.

"Strange, isn't she?" Dale said to Barbara as she watched Taya ride away.

Eric stood rooted in place and watched as she disappeared down the street while Sean and Brian started toward the house.

"Come on, Eric," Barbara called out to her son.

Eric looked toward his mother then back and saw Taya turn down the street.

✝

"Bedtime, you guys, brush your teeth, ten minutes okay?"

"Okay, Mom," both Eric and Sean said at the same time.

After getting ready for bed, both boys went into their own rooms to wait for their mother to come and tuck them in.

Barbara checked all the windows and doors downstairs and turned the security system on. She then went up the staircase and into Sean's room first.

"Did you brush your teeth?"

"Yes, Mom."

Barbara kissed him on the forehead and tucked him snugly tight. "Good night, sweetheart."

"Night, Mama," Sean said as he yawned.

Barbara turned on the night-light and partially closed his bedroom door before proceeding to Eric's room.

"Hey, my little man. Did you brush your teeth?"

"Yep."

Barbara sat down on Eric's bed as she had done with Sean.

"You okay? You seemed really quiet at dinner," Barbara asked as she brushed his hair lovingly away from his face with her fingers.

"Yeah…"

"What are you thinking about? Hmmmm?"

"About Taya."

Barbara was surprised. "What about her, honey?"

"If she dies no one will be sad," Eric said pensively.

Barbara looked away from her son for a moment. "I'm sure she must have someone, Eric," Barbara said, looking toward her son again, trying to reassure him.

Eric thought too much. Barbara had been worried about him for a long time now. She had ended her marriage with Jeff sooner rather than later because of the way Eric reacted whenever they had fought. Eric had always seen things too clearly. When she called him her little man she really did see him that way. And somehow thinking that hurt. Barbara wanted more than anything for her son to have a childhood—something that was constantly being challenged. So she would try to soothe his concerns and make him see other things that would not haunt him so.

"No, Mama, I don't think she does," Eric said as he looked deeply into his mother's eyes. Barbara caressed his angelic face.

"How can you be so sure?"

"Because she rides her motorcycle."

"But, Eric…"

"She's your friend now, right?"

"Well…"

"She kept looking at you when you weren't looking."

"She did?"

"Yeah."

"It's late, Eric, and you have school tomorrow," Barbara said as she tucked him. "Good night, honey."

"Maybe you should tell her not to ride the bike anymore, Mama."

"Good night, Eric," Barbara said as she turned off the light and pulled his door partway shut.

"Night, Mom. I love you."

Barbara smiled from out in the hallway and answered, "I love you too, sweetheart."

✝

Barbara went downstairs to make herself a cup of tea. She wore a silk peach two-piece pajama with a robe on top. As usual, she walked without her shoes, which had been an issue with Jeff. But now she did as she pleased. This was her house and she would walk around it barefoot if she wanted, and she did.

She took her tea and went to sit in the spacious family room. This was Barbara's favorite room in the house. She had decorated it in colors of peach and cream. Jeff had hated it. The house was to impress he had told her, but she had stuck to having this room the way she liked. This was supposed to be a home, after all, and the family room was where her family would spend most of their time. In the end, Jeff had relented. They would entertain in the more formal part of the house and she would be allowed to have her family room her way. Everything with Jeff had been a negotiation, Barbara realized. She sat down on an overstuffed sofa and for the first time that day allowed herself to try and make some sense out of what had been happening in her life lately.

Barbara looked around the room and saw the details that made this a home for her and her sons. There were little things that they had made for her on the shelves. There were photos of the boys from last Christmas and when they were babies. Books on a variety of subjects that she had been interested in and books that she read to her sons. As she looked around at the overstuffed pillows and the throw blankets she remembered the contrast to where Taya lived. Taya lived with a need for nothing. That was the best way to describe it. There was a barrenness in her life that was mirrored in how she lived. And suddenly it struck her that the sparseness of Taya's surroundings was self-imposed.

Chapter Six

The Iron Monster rode through the streets of the pens, searching. The air was thick with moisture and the streets were sizzling with the heat of half-covered women offering their wares for the right price. Heads turned as they saw the Black Angel ride by. Taya was looking for some way to release the raging emotions that seemed to throw energy out of her body.

She had checked with Stanley and all the white was on the street. She was meeting a new supplier in a few days. Her supplier from Colombia was getting too greedy. She had never liked him in the first place so a part of her was glad to end the partnership.

She was meeting with Rico Rivera. He was Cuban. That she understood. At least she could better understand the nuances and the lingo. Cuba…such a foreign concept now. When she had first gotten to the United States, over twenty-five years ago, it was all she thought about and all she heard about at home.

That was a long time ago, she told herself. Another lifetime…

What mattered was that the powder was on the street. Now, she was wound tight. Her nerves were on edge and she needed to release some of that energy. So she rode through the pens looking for what might satisfy for the night. She was so hungry for Barbara that she could taste it in her mouth. And no one…no one would control her like that.

The wheels of the bike rolled from one street to the other and on a corner she saw something that would do. She pulled up to the curb and looked the young woman over from top to bottom.

"Get on."

The young blonde looked toward someone in the dark alley, who stepped out quickly. As soon as he saw the Black Angel he nodded.

"Do whatever she wants," the pimp said to the young woman. "Whatever she wants, you hear, girl?"

The girl turned toward the other two older-looking women with some concern.

"That's Black Angel…just let her do whatever she wants or she'll get too rough," one of the women said to the girl low enough not to be overheard.

"Belinda!" The pimp hollered. "Don't make her wait. Go!"

Belinda got on the motorcycle and they sped away.

✝

Taya shoved the door open and it banged loudly against its frame. Belinda followed her inside the darkened room.

"Shut the door," Taya shouted.

Taya removed her coat and threw it over a chair. She walked toward her bedroom in the dark, not turning a single light on.

"Get in here!"

Belinda walked slowly, trying to maneuver in total darkness. When she walked in she heard the bedroom door bang shut behind her and turned in total fear.

"It's only me," Taya purred. She grabbed the girl by the front of her blouse and pulled her roughly toward the bed.

"Is that your real hair color?"

Belinda seemed to be surprised by Taya's question. "Yes," she replied.

Taya touched it for a moment, remembering another head of hair. Belinda could see Taya's face from the light of the moon coming through the window. She remained still as she saw the blade that glinted in the moonlight coming closer to her.

"Don't fight me and I won't hurt you," Taya said between her clenched teeth.

Belinda nodded.

"How long have you worked for Julian?" Taya asked as the blade of the knife lightly caressed Belinda's neck.

"About six months."

"You like your work?" Taya asked softly.

"I do all right."

The silver blade flew through the air and sliced down the front of Belinda's blouse.

"Jesus, I would have taken it off," Belinda complained.

Taya struck her across the face and Belinda fell on the bed. "You live by my will."

The young blonde lay on the bed and watched as Taya removed her boots, then her pants and strapped on the harness that she had pulled out of a drawer. She still held the knife in one hand.

"Get up!"

"I'll do whatever you want, okay." Belinda said, trying to placate the angry woman in front of her.

"Oh, you'll do whatever I want all right," was all Taya said as she turned Belinda around and tore off the rest of her clothes and bent her over.

✝

Barbara woke with a start. She looked around the room and realized she had fallen asleep on the sofa.

Taya…Barbara wondered and the name immediately left her lips. "Taya."

She picked up her teacup from the small table to leave in the kitchen and then went up to bed.

†

At that same moment Taya imagined Barbara's face and fucked the girl harder. She wanted to give pain. She wanted to give pain to release her own. That would take care of things. She got a better grip on the blonde's hips and began to fuck her harder and harder until the woman cried out in pain. Taya ignored her cries and kept fucking her until the girl was almost unconscious. She grabbed the blonde by the hair and pumped harder and harder. She never felt the rush of pleasure. It never came. She pushed the woman away from her in anger and lay down on the bed.

"Get out of here!"

Belinda was relieved that it was finally over but remembered that she was supposed to have pleased the Black Angel. If Julian thought for one moment that she had not done everything she could to satisfy the Black Angel he would kill her. Belinda had no doubts about that.

"I can do anything else you want. I can make you come by sucking you," Belinda said seductively as she tried to touch Taya's midriff. The blade flew through the air and cut the woman on the arm.

"No one touches me. Get out!"

Taya made like she was getting up and Belinda grabbed her tattered clothes and ran out of the apartment, thanking the Almighty for getting her out of there alive. She held onto her arm as blood began to trickle down it.

Taya removed her harness. Sweating, she lay back on the bed still wanting. Her body had felt no satisfaction since she had last been with Barbara. "Damn you to hell, Barbara. I should have just fucked you!" She pulled her gun out of its holster from the nightstand and began to fire randomly into the darkness.

All heads turned at the shots heard throughout the pens and all knew the anger of the roar that followed.

With the mighty roar the pens all came to life. They knew the lion was hungry and when that happened…death would inevitably follow.

✝

Taya lay in the dark. She could hear her own heavy breathing. She got up and walked over to her coat in the other room and pulled out something from its side pocket. She went back and lay down the bed again.

She pulled open the tab and the phone pad lit up. She dialed a number and waited.

"Hello?" said a sleepy voice from the other end.

"Good night, Barbara," Taya said softly.

"Goodnight, Taya."

Taya closed the cover of the cell phone and then closed her eyes.

Chapter Seven

Rico Rivera had been around for a few years. Unlike most suppliers he had lasted. He was reputed to deliver the white clean and that was rare. Rico was not the forgiving sort but was also known to honor a deal. Taya had been reluctant to negotiate with the Cuban. Too close to home, she had told herself, but sometimes change was required, and in the jungle of the pens change is what kept one on top and alive.

Taya set up a meeting with Rico in West New York, a small town in Hudson County, New Jersey. Once upon a time, Cubans had been the majority in the area, but with the years the tides had changed yet again. Now it was mainly North Americans, but that was okay, still plenty of Cubans around. She had not visited often but it was a place that she and Rico could blend in and not be noticed. They agreed to meet at Las Palmas, a restaurant known for its Cuban cuisine. As soon as Taya walked in the smells of her childhood flooded her mind.

She looked around, heard her native language being spoken at every turn, and she had to admit it felt good. It had been so long. She could smell the food, see the rush, hear the expressions and witness the attributes known only to her people. For a moment she forgot why she had come and a smile appeared on her face.

The smile did not last long, however, as it also opened a door she had not wanted opened again. For a brief moment the pain touched her. After all, that was a life she had walked away from. She was not remembered, nor did she want to be remembered.

"Vete! Vete lejos de aquí!" Her mother yelled at her to go far away.

"Mamá..." Taya felt the sting of those words as they cut her very soul.

"No, vete!" Her mother turned her back to her and began to cry.

A young Taya walked out of the house never to come back again.

Those were memories she did not want. That was a life she had left behind. It had been made clear that her family didn't want her and she didn't need them. She had other things to think of, she told herself. She was no longer that young woman. Taya had learned to live on the street and the scars of those lessons were not only present on her body but were also permanently on her soul. The girl she had been was long gone. Black Angel had taken her place. Taya looked around the restaurant again and put her past where it belonged, in the past. Why think about something that meant nothing?

She had made the reservation for eight p.m., but she was early. Taya told the hostess she wanted a quiet table on the corner to the right. She was seated, choosing to sit with her back to the wall, and ordered the expected rum and Coke. As soon as Rico entered the restaurant she saw him. Within seconds he was by her side. No need for introductions. It would have been insulting to pretend. Taya stood and they shook hands. Rico sat down opposite Taya and ordered rum and Coke, or as it was known to them, a "Cuba Libre."

"*La comida Cubana aquí es excelente*," Rico commented on the restaurant's food.

Their conversation would be in their own language.

"Yes, the food here is great," Taya went straight into it as well.

"I hope that we do business for a long time. I am especially happy to do business with a fellow Cuban," Rico said as he took his glass and raised it.

Taya raised hers as well and they toasted to the beginning of a profitable future.

"How much?"

"You cut right to the chase, *mija*," Rico commented with a smile.

"That's why we're here. How much per kilo?"

Rico wrote a figure on his napkin.

"That's too much."

"It costs us a lot, Taya. I can let you have it for this…" He wrote on the napkin again. "Being my *compatriota* this is a special offer just for you."

"Still too much."

The waitress approached them. "Are you ready to order?"

"*Arroz con pollo*," Rico enthusiastically ordered chicken and rice. "They really do it justice here," he pointed out to Taya.

"I'll have the same with a side order of *plátanos maduros*." She could not resist ordering the sweet fried plantains.

"Give me an order of those as well," Rico added.

The waitress left them and Rico sat back and looked at Taya, leaving no doubt what he was thinking.

"It's good to do business with your own kind," Rico said, raising his glass again.

"Yes, we both know what the other is capable of," Taya said, smiling back.

"I see why they call you Black Angel," Rico laughed. "You are definitely lovely."

"I'm the last face they see. I hope my name does not define our new...friendship," Taya said and suddenly the smile was gone. What Rico saw in those eyes made him sit up. In that moment he realized all the stories he had heard were true. In front of him, staring at him now were the eyes of a cold-blooded killer and, if the stories were true, a brilliant one.

Rico nodded and they got down to business. They agreed on a price and to an exchange of risk. This may work out after all, Taya thought to herself by the end of the night.

"Your family, they all here in the United States?" Rico asked as he was eating.

Taya immediately looked him straight in the eyes. As soon as he saw her reaction he stopped chewing.

"You deal with me!" she growled through her teeth.

"*Oye, Taya, cálmate consorte!*" Rico tried calming her down.

"*Tú y yo,*" she said, her face within an inch of his. "You try to fuck me and I will cut off your balls and shove them down your throat," she growled.

She pulled away slowly and then purred. "A toast, Rico. To money...to lots of it." She raised her glass. And then she added something unexpected, "And to *Cuba libre.*"

"*Cuba libre.*" Rico raised his glass and the partnership was solidified with the last part of the toast. After all, they were the same kind. He admired the fact that she was tough. As a partner she would probably last. They also shared an old struggle and that, in a very real way, bound them. In sharing that, there was strength and from that they could build.

✝

As soon as Taya road into her territory she could smell trouble. She could feel the tension as she passed the shadows. At that moment the Iron Monster roared and Taya headed for the new cutting room.

She walked into the safe house where a newly arrived batch of rock candy—what names!—was being bagged. But the candy was flying out and the cash was pouring in. It was quickly becoming more popular than heroin, and cheaper. The more the customers got the more they wanted, and that was, as they say, 'good for business.' Her powder didn't have any junk in it and for that assurance people paid.

Taya walked around the tables and saw that the packages were being weighed properly. She always made sure to make eye contact with both the cutters and the ones that weighed it. In that one look they understood that if something went wrong Black Angel would know what they looked like.

Stanley approached her after she finished her inspection. "Taya, can I have a minute?"

Taya nodded and they walked over to a small room that had a few chairs and a table in it. Taya sat and Stanley followed.

"Who's dead?" she asked as she took out a cigarette and lit it.

Stanley stared at her for a moment then began to speak. "Nico…Julian sliced him up but good. He took over his girls."

"Julian, the one that has Broadway and Pulaski Highway, right?" Taya said as she took a drag off her cigarette.

"Yeah. His stable covers both streets," Stanley confirmed.

Taya took another drag and remained quiet.

"And?" Taya finally asked.

"He sent word that you would understand…that you both had an understanding. I didn't want to do anything until I spoke with you." Stanley waited patiently.

Fuck! Taya thought to herself trying to keep her anger in check. That stupid motherfucker. She took another drag from her cigarette as Stanley waited patiently.

"He said he has what you want and it's yours to do with as you will. I was to give you that message." Stanley had heard some talk about one of the prostitutes but he was not about to acknowledge knowing anything.

Nico had crossed the line. He was making a move and it had to be dealt with quickly and efficiently. Order kept the wolves at bay…and Julian had kicked in the door.

Taya got up and opened the door. "Christopher! Come here." She stepped back in the room and closed it behind the man who had sprinted over.

"You have been with me for a long time," she said as she put the cigarette out.

"Yes, Taya. I started on South Street and now I've been on the north delivery route for about two years."

"Good. Stanley, get Pete and Martin. We're going to pay Julian a visit. And Christopher…you ride with me." She walked out of the room and immediately both men sprang into action.

✝

Three black cars pulled up and cut off any possible escape for Julian. Taya rode straight up to him. The Iron Monster roared loudly before she silenced it and dismounted. Christopher got off with her, and stood right behind her.

"Taya…good to see you," Julian said nervously. Some of the girls that were close by took a few steps back to get closer to the wall and farther away from Julian.

"You say you have something of mine, *cabrón*?" Taya said menacingly as she got closer to him.

"Taya, no! I said that she was yours, Taya. Everything of mine is yours." Julian was beginning to tremble.

"You don't have anything I want, you motherfucker!"

"Taya, I just meant that you seemed to like Belinda and…"

"I fucked a whore. And you think that entitles you to take something without asking me first?" Taya took out her blade and Julian took a step back. He began to sweat, droplets appearing across his forehead.

"Taya, I meant no disrespect…I thought you liked her. She is one of my best earners. She is yours, Taya. You can fuck her to death…she is yours. I know you enjoyed fucking her. Jesus, Taya…I didn't mean anything by it." Julian was close to falling apart.

"You insult me, Julian. Are you suggesting that I deserve a whore?" Taya began playing with the blade in her hand.

"Fuck, Taya, don't do it, man. Please don't. I didn't mean to offend you," he begged.

Taya walked up to him. She looked him straight in the eye. "But you did offend me, Julian," she said softly then walked away from him.

Everyone's eyes were on Taya as she got back on her bike until they heard a gurgle from Julian. They watched his body as it fell to the ground. As he lay there, red quickly spread across his once white shirt. Taya simply put her blade in her jacket.

"Stanley," Taya said and he was immediately at her side. "Dust to dust." She smiled and Stanley nodded. "And Stanley, Christopher will take over Julian's and Nico's stables now."

Stanley looked at a surprised Christopher.

"Taya, thank you. I will be loyal, Taya," Christopher added quickly.

"I know you will. Give Stanley his tribute. Always remember who you serve and the pens will run smoothly."

Christopher nodded and Stanley suddenly understood the brilliance of the move. They would all profit. Taya was becoming even more of a mystery to him. She was diabolically brilliant and he was glad that he was on her good side. All her actions had a purpose. There was no emotion in her at all. Christopher had been rewarded and he would also profit. There was no loss. Julian had made the mistake of making it personal and a lesson had been taught for all to hear loud and clear.

Chapter Eight

It had been a difficult morning. Eric had woke up with a slight fever due to a cold so Barbara had asked Jean to take over the carpool to the lower school that morning. Eric was resting in the family room, wrapped in his favorite blanket, watching the morning cartoons. Barbara had gone to the kitchen to get the Tylenol Cold to give Eric a dose. She hadn't been feeling like herself for a while now either. She looked down at the Tylenol bottle and wished there was something she could take to stop the ache she felt inside.

Barbara had been preoccupied since she received that very disturbing call from Taya a few nights before. The call had caught her off guard, but it seemed so natural to just say goodnight. The incident was very present in her thoughts this morning. Of course, it didn't help matters that Dale was grilling her every day about what seemed to be going on.

The doorbell rang and Barbara walked over to answer it, the Tylenol bottle still in her hand. This time it did not catch her by surprise to find Taya standing there.

"Hi," Taya said softly, almost shyly.

"Hi," Barbara replied, smiling, surprising even herself. She looked at Taya in some detail for a moment. Somehow it seemed important to notice all the details of the woman in front of her.

"Can I come in, *querida*?" Taya then asked huskily and waited.

Barbara stepped aside. Words didn't seem important at that moment. She closed the door and turned to face Taya. There was a silent understanding in what was not being said, as if words held no meaning. Barbara fought the part of her that just wanted to look at the beautiful creature in front of her and not question why or why not.

"Tylenol?" Taya smiled a little as she took off her sunglasses and looked deeper into Barbara's eyes.

"Oh…" Barbara seemed to snap out of her momentary trance. "Eric has a slight fever."

"I have a cold," a small voice said from behind them.

Taya turned around and looked down.

"Hi, Taya." Eric smiled.

"Hello, sir. I hear you're sick." She knelt down in front of the boy.

"Yeah…" he said and sneezed.

"God bless you," Barbara and Taya said simultaneously.

Eric giggled. Taya got up and laughed too.

"Hey, you like cartoons?" he asked enthusiastically.

"Cartoons?" Taya asked.

"Yeah, Cat and Dog is on. Come on, that one is my favorite." Eric grabbed her by the hand and began pulling. Taya smiled at Barbara who shook her head and smiled back.

Taya spent most of the morning watching cartoons with Eric. She found him to be a very bright and intriguing child. Were most boys his age like this? No…he was definitely not like most boys, Taya told herself.

Eric loved the attention, of course, but it was more than that, Barbara told herself later. Taya really listened to his detailed explanations about the most incredible things. Eric looked at her adoringly as she commented on things. Taya talked to him not at him or down to him. That was something she had never been able to explain to Jeff. Taya had managed to surprise her yet again. As much as Barbara tried to put her in a box Taya just never seemed to fit into it. She was like a chameleon. Every time Barbara saw her there was yet another aspect to this most intriguing woman.

Barbara was in the kitchen making Eric some soup for lunch when she heard laughter coming from the family room. Real laughter…deep and wonderful. She had not heard Eric laugh like that for so long. It felt good to hear him laugh like that again, and it warmed Barbara's heart. Taya, the last person she would have expected, had made that happen.

Taya was more of an enigma to her than ever. She was someone who had come into her life and seemed to be quickly becoming a piece of it. When Barbara walked into the family room about fifteen minutes later to call them for lunch she was surprised by what she found.

Taya had not heard her approaching. Eric had his head on her lap and was asleep. Barbara leaned silently against the doorframe and watched as Taya caressed her son's golden locks. She seemed so gentle at that moment as she caressed Eric lovingly. Taya then pulled the blanket to cover him better and smiled at the sleeping little boy.

At that moment Barbara's heart gave an extra beat. When Taya looked up Barbara saw her eyes were soft and unguarded. Barbara looked back at her with such tenderness that it touched Taya's very soul. For a moment many things were said between them and yet not a word was spoken.

Barbara smiled and walked over toward them, helping Taya get up slowly so as not to wake up Eric. Taya was about to speak when she put her finger softly over her mouth.

Both women walked to the kitchen in silence.

"I made some soup. Do you like soup?" Barbara asked with the most delightful smile Taya had ever seen on any woman's face.

"Yes," was all she was able to say. Her heart was beating faster and faster and she felt as excited and jumpy as a child at the same time.

"Sit down. I'll get you some," Barbara said, touching her arm briefly before walking over to the stove.

Taya's eyes followed Barbara as she sat down.

Barbara set the bowl of split pea soup in front of Taya. She got some utensils from the drawer close by.

"Are you having lunch with me?" Taya asked hopefully.

"Yes." Barbara smiled and went to get another bowl.

"It's good," Taya said as she looked up.

"Thank you."

They ate the rest of their lunch in silence. When they were done Barbara began to pick up the plates and as she was retrieving the bowl in front of Taya, she found her hand had been taken.

"Barbara," Taya said as she pulled Barbara down to her slowly. Their lips met for a light kiss. Such a small thing and yet it spoke volumes.

Barbara straightened up.

"I came to give you this," Taya said as she stood up next to Barbara and pulled a piece of paper from her pocket.

Barbara put the bowl back down on the table and unfolded the white piece of paper. She read the contents and looked up at Taya.

"I'm sorry it took me a few days," Taya said, staring down at her boots.

"Thank you," Barbara said softly as she looked at the dark head of the woman staring at the floor in front of her.

Taya felt a hand close to her face and instinctively pulled away. She was looking straight at Barbara now. Again Barbara reached out, slowly, to touch her face. This time Taya stood still.

"I don't but, I better go understand you," Barbara said softly as she caressed the face of the woman before her.

Taya felt the light caress and her eyes closed as she leaned her face into it. When Taya's eyes opened again Barbara saw all of the passion and desire that Taya had for her in those eyes. She took a step toward it and her mouth came up beckoning, expecting.

"Barbara?" A voice brought them back to reality.

Taya immediately took a step away from Barbara as Dale walked into the kitchen. Dale stared at them with the certainty that she had walked in on something. Barbara looked like she wanted to hide and visibly paled. Taya just looked away.

"I…hi," Dale said uncomfortably.

Barbara ran her fingers through her hair as she put more distance between her and Taya.

"I came to see how Eric was doing…is everything okay?" Dale asked as she looked from one woman to the other.

"Yeah, I was just leaving," Taya said quickly, not looking at anyone in particular. "Thanks for lunch." She wanted to put as much space as possible between her and Barbara. Something was happening…something had happened and she couldn't or didn't want to face it.

Taya grabbed her coat and turned to leave.

"Wait! You don't have to go…I have some…" Barbara suddenly stopped talking and stared at Taya as she turned and faced her. "You don't have to go," she added softly.

"Thanks, but, I better go," Taya said and smiled. She walked over to Barbara, leaned down, kissed her on the cheek close to her ear, and whispered as she pulled away. "Goodbye *querida mía.*"

Taya looked into Barbara's eyes for a moment and smiled, then turned to leave.

"Nice to see you again, Dale," Taya said as she walked past her.

Dale stared at Taya as she left, then turned back to Barbara.

"Okay, you wanna tell me what the hell is going on here?" Barbara began to tell her when Eric walked in.

"Hi, Aunt Dale," said a sleepy little boy. "Where is Taya, Mama?"

†

Taya walked into her apartment. She stood in the middle of her small living room for the better part of thirty minutes just thinking, remembering, regretting and then she took a deep breath, closed her eyes and let her head fall back.

Straightening up, she walked over to the sofa and sat down, her coat still on. "Damn. Damn. Damn," she said to herself as she leaned her head back on the sofa and closed her eyes again. After a moment she sat up and leaned forward holding both her hands. "I should have known better…God!" She covered her face with her hands, trying to hide the woman within from what she could no longer hide even from herself.

"Are you having lunch with me?" Taya ridiculed herself. "Jesus Christ! I acted like a…what the fuck is wrong with me?"

†

Barbara had taken Eric back to the family room. When she returned to the kitchen she saw Dale reading the paper Taya had brought her.

Dale looked up immediately and Barbara froze on the spot.

"Barbara?" Dale held out the piece of paper.

Barbara walked over and took it from her. She folded it and put it in the pocket of her slacks.

"Barbara?"

"What Dale? What?" Barbara turned toward her sister.

"Explain."

"Why? Why do I have to explain this or anything to you?" Barbara said angrily. "I love you, Dale, but frankly this is none of your business. Stay out of it!" Barbara turned and started getting a tray for Eric.

Dale was silent as Barbara prepared the tray for Eric's lunch. She sat down, trying to figure out what to say or not to say, or whether she should say anything at all!

Barbara took the tray to Eric and came back to find Dale still sitting in the kitchen.

"Barb?" Dale spoke softly. "It's a VD/AIDS test."

"Yes, it is, Dale." Barbara faced it straight on. "And none of your business."

"Barbara…when I came in…" Dale spoke slowly, waiting to see her sister's reaction.

"Do you want lunch, Dale?" Barbara did not look away for a moment. And that was more frightening than asking the questions that were dancing around in her mind.

"Yes, thanks, I do."

"Good, lunch I can do." Barbara turned to get another bowl of soup.

✝

"I don't understand this obsession you seem to have with Barbara's life. So you found a VD/AIDS test, Dale. She was probably afraid that Jeff might have given her something. She was just being responsible and finding out if she was infected or something," Rob argued.

"Rob, it wasn't her test," Dale explained to her husband.

"What do you mean? Whose was it then?"

"She has this new friend. Her name is Taya, it was her test, and…I don't know. I can't really figure it out. Barbara said they met at counseling."

"Barbara is going to counseling?"

"That's just it…it doesn't add up. She says she is, but she never said anything to me about it. This whole thing with Jeff has her acting strangely. And Taya is, well…she seems nice enough, but, at the same time, there is something about her that scares me a little."

"Why do you think that is, sweetheart?" Rob walked over to his wife and took her in his arms.

"Taya just doesn't seem like the type of person that Barbara usually makes friends with. I worry about her, Rob. She's my kid sister. I have always looked out for her."

"I know, sweetheart, but Barbara is a big girl. I would bet this whole thing with Jeff has made her rethink a lot of things."

"Yes, you're probably right. My mind is working overtime, huh?" Dale smiled and looked up.

Rob leaned down and kissed her lightly on the lips.

"You love her and you worry, that's just you."

Chapter Nine

Muffled sounds roused her out of a sound sleep. Getting up, she felt the cold floor beneath her feet. She was always cold now since coming to the United States. Getting the blanket from her bed she put it over her shoulders and tiptoed slowly toward the raised voices coming from outside her room.

She opened the door slightly. Through the crack she could see her older sister sitting on the sofa and her mother crying. Fear filled her small body, as it had before they had come to get them that night in Cuba, a few days before they came to America. There had been crying then too. Her grandmother had told her mother in no uncertain terms that she must go and take her children to freedom…the opportunity might not come again. Her mother had been crying then too. Taya missed her grandmother. There were a lot of good things in the United States, but it wasn't home. She was always cold and her father was not the same.

Keeping quiet, she tried to listen. From the corner of her eye she could see her father.

"I don't love you anymore," her father said bluntly. "I want Dolores."

"The children, Tomás, what about the children?" her mother asked as she wept.

"Dolores is pregnant," he blurted out. "I'm sorry."

"And our children? What about them? You promised me that if I came to America you would leave her and we would be a family. I believed you, Tomás!"

"I can't divorce her. She's my wife. You always knew that!"

"Taya won't understand," her mother emphasized. "She doesn't know."

"Dolores was not able to give me children in Cuba. But now she is pregnant." He made it sound like that was all that mattered. Saying nothing else, he walked out.

Her mother tried to go after him, but her sister Laura stopped her. "Mama, we don't need him. Let him go. He doesn't want us, Mama! Let him go with that whore…we will be just fine without him."

"Laura, you all need a father. Francisco is already getting in trouble and your sister is headstrong. I don't want you to have to leave school," her mother said between tears.

"Mama, he's gone. We're on our own. And we will survive just fine. He has never loved us, Mama."

"Taya will not understand. She adores him."

"Taya will be just fine. I will talk to her. We don't have to tell her that he has abandoned us, Mama, she will be fine," Laura tried to reassure her mother.

Closing the door Taya went back to bed. She stared at the ceiling till morning. Laura tried talking to her the next morning but she didn't want to listen. Taya never asked about her father again and they never tried to talk to her about it. They all thought it was better that way.

Taya was awake most of the night; memories seemed to be coming to her from all directions. Memories that she thought were long forgotten. Memories that still hurt. As much as she told herself she was no longer that young girl…something inside her still felt the pain. As she had done that night long ago, she stared at the ceiling all night. Suddenly it became important to move. She got up quickly and began to dress. She would have breakfast with Barbara.

Taya flew through the pens. She didn't want to think about why she was running to Barbara. All she knew was that seeing Barbara would make her stop hurting. Fighting this attraction was less important than dulling the pain of the endless pit inside her. When she was with Barbara she didn't think, she didn't remember, she didn't have to be constantly looking to see where the next blow was coming from. In Barbara she found some peace. She didn't think about all this, of course, she just hurt and Barbara, for now, was the painkiller.

She was ringing Barbara's doorbell within forty-five minutes. Impatient, Taya rang the bell again. When the door opened and she saw the blond woman in front of her she was able to breathe more calmly.

"Are you alone? Can I come in?"

Barbara nodded. Taya walked into the middle of the living room then turned around. Barbara stood nearby and watched, sensing that something was wrong. Taya removed her sunglasses and slowly walked to her, scanning Barbara's face as if searching for something.

Taya was lost for a moment, unsure what to do now that she was with Barbara. Barbara embraced her gently. Taya stood stock still, arms hanging at her sides, wanting yet not daring to return the embrace. After a moment her head dropped to Barbara's shoulder and her arms wrapped around her. When she felt Barbara's embrace tighten, her body began to shake and the tears began slowly, gradually turning into sobs. Barbara held her tightly and caressed her hair gently.

†

Taya woke up to noise. She sat up quickly, looking around in confusion. Then she remembered how she and Barbara had sat on the sofa. She must have cried herself to sleep in Barbara's arms.

"Eric, give me the control. I can get that fireball for you," Sean insisted.

"I can do it myself, Sean. Don't be so loud, you're going to wake up Taya."

"Taya's awake."

Both boys turned around and ran over to her, the video game forgotten.

"Did we wake you up?" Sean asked as a mischievous smile formed.

"Hmmm…" She tried to look censorious.

"I'm sorry, Taya." Sean looked a bit remorseful.

"Don't worry about it, kid. What are you playing over there anyway?"

"It's a video game. We are saving the galaxy from alien invaders," Eric said enthusiastically.

"Never played a video game," Taya said thoughtfully.

Sean and Eric looked at one another then back at Taya.

"Wanna play?" Eric asked as he jumped on the sofa to sit next to her.

"I'll teach you. I'm really good at this game," Sean interrupted.

"Yeah, sure." Taya sat on the floor as Sean handed her the hand control.

"You put your fingers here."

†

"They woke you up, huh?" Barbara asked as she leaned on the doorframe.

Three sets of eyes looked up at her from the floor.

"Oh no, I woke up all by myself." Taya, Sean, and Eric smiled at one another. "I'm fighting the alien invaders."

"I can see that." Barbara smiled. "Dinner will be ready in about fifteen minutes." She turned around to leave when Taya called out to her.

"Barbara?"

Barbara turned toward her again.

"Thank you."

Barbara smiled. "You're welcome. I hope you like fettuccine Alfredo."

"Yeah, I do."

"Good, now hurry up and save the world. Dinner is almost ready."

Taya smiled as Barbara walked away. *What is it about her?*

"Taya! They're coming!"

Taya turned toward the TV. "Get those nukes ready, Sean."

✝

That night, as Taya lay in her bed, she remembered the day and smiled. It had been so long since she had just felt good. It wasn't that she didn't like kids, she did, but kids were generally boring. Eric and Sean were different, though, she told herself. They were smart, funny, and they were great to be with. They all had dinner together and it was like nothing she had ever experienced. Barbara and the kids talked about things like history and documentaries. What had impressed her the most was how much they obviously loved each other. And the most unexpected thing of all was how they had included her.

Yeah, they're great kids. How could they not be; every time she looked at them she saw Barbara in their eyes?

Taya picked up her cell phone and dialed.

"Hello?"

"Good night, Barbara," Taya said softly.

"Good night, Taya. Sleep well."

She closed the cell phone and smiled softly into the darkness. For the first time in a very long time Taya closed her eyes and slept soundly. No nightmares came to haunt her that night; only rest, much needed rest.

Chapter Ten

As Taya pulled up on her bike, Christopher walked over to her.

"Taya, anything I can do for you?" he asked, looking toward the girls.

Taya leaned forward and smiled. Belinda stared back at her and smiled, her importance having grown as she kept telling the story of how she had been fought over.

"No, thanks. How are things going? Any trouble?"

"Nothing I can't handle. Business is good." Christopher smiled.

"Words I love to hear. Later." Taya's Iron Monster roared as she rode away. Belinda's eyes followed her.

"Hey, I thought you were her woman, B?"

"I'm supposed to meet her later, Casey," Belinda barked back defensively.

"They say she has an upscale piece of ass now."

"Who said that?"

"That's the word on the street. What I heard was that Jake tried to touch that piece of ass and he kind of went into lala land, if you know what I mean." Casey raised her eyebrows.

"That was before me," Belinda argued.

"Didn't look like she was interested to me." Casey laughed as she walked away.

Belinda walked over to Christopher. "Chris, I have to leave early tonight."

"And why is that?"

"Taya wants me."

"Didn't say anything to me about it."

"You wanna have her come get me 'cause I'm not there later?" Belinda mouthed off.

"All right. You can split early."

Belinda smiled like the cat that swallowed the canary. She knew what Taya liked and she would use that. Taya was her ticket off the corner.

✝

"Hi," Taya said when Barbara opened the door.

Barbara smiled. "Hi, come on in."

"I got these new games for Sean and Eric. The guy at Toys R Us said they were the latest," Taya said as she walked into the house.

"They're with their father. He picked them up about thirty minutes ago."

"Oh."

"They spend every other weekend with him. Well, when he is available anyway."

"Well, here," Taya handed her the shopping bag, "the guy at the store said these were the most popular games. I thought that, well, maybe they would like them." Taya seemed more uncomfortable by the second.

"I'm sure they will love them. Thank you."

"Do you have any plans for dinner?" Taya asked, looking away though her sunglasses were still on.

"Just eating," Barbara said jokingly.

"You like Chinese?" Taya asked as she gazed down at her boots.

"Yes."

"You wanna go with me, maybe?" Taya kept staring at her boots.

Barbara smiled. "Are you asking me out on a date?"

Taya looked up immediately, but said nothing. Then to Barbara's surprise Taya nodded. "Do you want to?" The words came out with a little uncertainty.

"Yes," Barbara answered softly.

Taya smiled a little then her face lit up from within. "Good."

✝

They decided that it was best to take Barbara's car since it looked like it might start to rain. They went to a Chinese restaurant in downtown Upper Montclair that Barbara had heard from Jean had excellent food.

For a few hours, without discussing it, neither woman spoke about how they had met or where they came from. They kept their conversation to light topics at first, but as they gradually grew more comfortable with each other, there were small gestures—brushes of hands, a glance—that spoke of a shared feeling that had no name and did not need to be verbalized. They each recognized something within the other that had called out to them.

Sometime during the evening Barbara realized, as she looked at Taya speaking, that this feeling was more than sexual. Taya was a mystery, gentleness, roughness and tenderness all rolled into one. And Taya was beautiful. Barbara stared at her hands for a moment and quickly looked away. Taya's hands were magic.

Taya was amazed how easy it was to talk to Barbara. What became the most obvious was how long it had been since she had talked to anyone as a friend. She didn't have to worry if there were any ulterior motives with Barbara because there weren't. And Barbara's eyes…she could get lost in Barbara's eyes. By the time they finished eating Taya was looking for any excuse to lengthen the time.

"I'll have to tell Dale and Mom about this place," Barbara commented.

"The food here is pretty good."

"Do you have any brothers or sisters?" Barbara asked out of nowhere. Taya froze at the question. Barbara waited patiently.

"Two. One brother and one sister." Taya shifted uncomfortably in her chair.

"Do you see them often?"

"No."

Barbara waited but Taya added nothing else.

Barbara sighed. "It's late, we better get going." Taya could tell that her brusque answers had upset Barbara somehow. But her family was an issue that she wasn't comfortable discussing.

"Do you want some dessert?"

"I don't think I can eat another thing," Barbara answered sullenly. "And it looks like the weather is getting worse." She looked out the window closest to her.

"Yeah, you're right. We better go." Taya got up and threw a few twenty-dollar bills on the table.

The drive back to the house was made in silence. When they pulled into the driveway and Barbara turned off the car she realized that Taya was staring straight ahead and didn't seem to want to move.

"Taya? Are you okay?" Barbara asked with concern apparent in her voice.

"I haven't seen them in over fifteen years."

Barbara sat quietly in the darkness that enveloped them inside the car and listened.

"Where are they?"

"In another world," Taya said sadly then turned to Barbara and, looking straight at her, added, "in your world."

"Taya…"

"Barbara, I can't…I don't want to talk about this. I was something they put out with the trash okay? I don't need them."

Barbara placed her hand on Taya's briefly before Taya pulled hers away. "I'm the person who doesn't get introduced at family functions. I'm the wrong sort, Barbara," she added with sarcasm. "Come on, I'll walk you in then I gotta go." Taya got out of the car quickly.

They walked up to the front door in silence. Barbara unlocked it and as she went in she turned around. Taya took a step closer and Barbara switched on the overhead light. Taya pulled back, getting the message loud and clear. They stood looking at each other for a moment in silence.

Barbara switched off the overhead light and Taya took her in her arms and kissed her passionately. Barbara pulled away and, still holding Taya's hand, pulled her inside and closed the door behind them.

"Are you sure?" Taya surprised herself by asking.

"Yes, I'm more than sure," Barbara said, returning Taya's passionate kiss with one of her own.

✝

"I want to look at you," Taya said as she stood by the nightstand.

Barbara nodded and Taya walked over and slowly began to unbutton Barbara's blouse all the while looking into those deep blue eyes. Suddenly she stopped and stared at Barbara for a moment.

"Your eyes…"

"Yes?"

"They're not blue."

"Yes, they are," Barbara said softly and smiled.

"No, they are different shades of green and blue surrounded by golden sparks," Taya elaborated.

Barbara raised her hand and touched Taya's face with a full heart. "Who are you?" she asked softly in wonder.

"Nobody," Taya whispered.

"You're somebody to me." Barbara walked into Taya's embrace and kissed her.

Their lovemaking was passionate but in between the blinding desire to satisfy there was tenderness and softness. They made love into the night. Both pleased and were pleased. Afterward, Barbara lay in Taya's embrace.

"Taya?"

"Yes?"

"I want to go inside you."

Barbara felt Taya stiffen then sit up in bed. Barbara sat up too.

"I have never let anyone touch me. When I told you there was no chance about the…it was because no one had ever…" Taya trailed off.

Barbara took in all the information in silence.

"You…"

"I have been the only one who has touched you? And my mouth has been…?"

"The only one," Taya said as she looked away. Why had she told Barbara? She didn't want this. She didn't want to be here.

Barbara wasn't sure how to react or what to say. This was something she had never expected from Taya. And perhaps that was what hit her the hardest. What did she really know about Taya?

"Taya…"

"I can't talk about this right now, Barbara." Taya got up and started to dress.

"You can't or you won't?"

"Fine then, I won't," Taya said flippantly.

I gotta get out of here, Taya told herself as she pulled on her boots.

"I'm just another fuck to you," Barbara said as she ran her fingers through her hair. "Jesus, don't I ever learn?"

Taya looked at the woman sitting on the bed. There were a million things she wanted to say and yet nothing was coming out of her mouth.

"Get out," Barbara said wearily.

"Barbara…"

"Just go."

Taya placed a card on the nightstand. "My cell number."

Barbara looked up at her. "You don't have a phone."

Taya did not look away as Barbara smiled and shook her head. "Of course you have a cell phone. You always did, didn't you?"

"Yes."

"God, just get out. Please get out," Barbara cried as she covered her face. Taya closed the door behind her and ran down the stairs and out the door.

As soon as Barbara heard the bike roar her anguish seemed to grow. Taya had taken all she wanted and now she was gone.

Chapter Eleven

Taya rode for hours. It didn't matter where she was going; she just wanted to feel the distance. Tears ran unchecked down her face. She told herself over and over again that it didn't matter, that Barbara was just a good fuck, but she knew it wasn't true. She had known from the very first moment she looked into those eyes that something inside her had shifted. And now, Barbara wanted in, inside her body, inside her life, inside her soul, and all those places Barbara could not be allowed to enter. What would she see? And how could Taya ever expect her to understand. She was what she was and nothing could ever change that.

Taya finally got to her apartment in the early morning hours. All the shadows of her past and her present seemed to be looming closer than usual. For the first time she didn't care if they enveloped her. She had made her choices and it was too late to change them now. She could no more be a part of Barbara's world than Barbara could be part of hers. And that left them both exactly nowhere.

She walked into the apartment, and looked around at the emptiness. For the first time she saw what Barbara must have seen. Emptiness, she was surrounded by emptiness. How long had she just existed? Where had the years gone? Taya asked herself.

A knock on her door interrupted her thoughts. Taya turned and pulled the door open. Caution was something that did not seem to matter at that moment. Belinda smiled as she stood in front of the Black Angel.

"I waited for you all night and most of the day," Belinda purred.

"I'm not aware we had an appointment," Taya said sarcastically.

"You look tense. I can relieve the ache that fills you."

Taya walked into the room and Belinda closed the door behind her. Sitting down, Taya stared at the blonde in front of her. She pulled out a cigarette and lit it as she watched Belinda. She took a long drag and let out the smoke slowly.

"Do you want it here?"

Taya kept staring and said nothing while she smoked.

"I can be very good to you. I will let you do anything," Belinda said as she walked closer.

"Why are you here?"

"I want to belong to the Black Angel," Belinda said seductively. "I want to be fucked raw by you, baby."

"And if I were nobody?" Taya asked.

Belinda seemed confused. "You are somebody. You are Black Angel. You are life and death."

Taya smiled ironically and put out her cigarette. With disgust written on her face she said, "Yes, I am life and death. I hurt someone today." Taya then pulled out her gun and put it on her lap, her finger on the trigger. Belinda froze. "Wanna play with life and death?" Taya asked her with a look of pure evil.

Belinda shook her head dumbly.

"Smart girl. Now get out of here."

Belinda grabbed the jacket she had put on the chair close by on her way out the door.

Chapter Twelve

Dale noticed that Barbara had been quieter than usual. There was a sadness about her that was undeniable.

Every time the phone rang Barbara almost seemed to dread picking it up. Dale had gotten several concerned calls from their mother.

"Dale, there is something wrong and she is not talking," Joan Barrett said.

"I know, Mom. I have tried to get her to talk to me but she won't budge. I'm getting worried about her."

"Do you think it's something to do with Jeff that she is not saying?"

"No. She did tell me about the hidden investments and all that. That upset her, but there is something else going on and she just won't talk," Dale said in frustration.

"I'm going over there right now. Barbara always was too stubborn," Joan told her oldest daughter. "I'll call you when I get back."

"Okay, Mom, good luck."

✝

Almost a week had gone by and Taya kept telling herself that this pain inside her would also pass. She picked up the phone many times only to put it away again. She, unlike the addicts of the white powder, would not allow this desire to become her master. She had no ties to anyone and she liked it that way. But the nights…the nights she had no control over. There Barbara would come to her each and every night, tempting her, touching her and making her wake up full of a need she was finding unbearable to live with.

✝

As much as Barbara dreaded the phone when it rang she longed to answer it, she had to admit that part of her felt a certain sadness every time she answered it and it was not Taya.

Barbara told herself over and over again that she would not look the other way like she had with Jeff. She wanted Taya. Her body reminded her of that every moment of every day. But Taya had too many secrets. There were too many possibilities for lies. When the moment presented itself Taya had turned and ran off. She'd had enough problems dealing with Jeff to want to get into a relationship with someone who was not willing to even discuss the most basic things. Taya guarded her life, her past, anything to do with the personal in a way that the only conclusion possible to a relationship with her was fear. A relationship? With Taya? Yes, Barbara had to admit she would have taken a chance. She had never felt what she felt for Taya with anyone, not even Jeff. That led her to the conclusion that yes, she would have taken a chance with Taya. Against all the odds she would have taken a chance. But, what chance could one possibly take with a ghost.

Barbara realized that's what Taya was, a ghost. She seemed to exist without rhyme or reason, without a past, a present, or a future. What kind of life could one have with someone who didn't seem to exist? Yet, Taya made her feel alive.

Barbara shook her head. It was best this way, she told herself over and over again. The ache would eventually cease and her life would go back to what it had been before, predictable.

At that moment the phone rang.

"Hello?"

"I need to see you," a voice filled with controlled passion whispered over the phone. Barbara didn't have to ask who it was. Taya's voice was unmistakable. It had been branded into her very being and it resided in a place that she could not reach so that she could tear it out.

"I can't do this, Taya. I don't want to." Barbara tried to convince even herself as she said the words.

"You know you like it when I touch you, *querida*." Taya's voice was seductive and it made Barbara close her eyes. "We can keep it simple. Just mutual satisfaction."

"Get a whore off a street corner," Barbara blurted and Taya could tell that what she had said had stung.

"Barbara…"

"No," Barbara answered softly.

"Please…" Taya's plea came as a whisper. There was a moment of silence. "Barbara…" Taya could not hide the emotion in her voice.

Does she want me as much as I want her? Barbara asked herself. She closed her eyes.

"I'm coming tonight." Suddenly Taya's voice turned to anger. "My body aches for you…I feel your mouth on my skin, Barbara. I am burning and I know that you are too." Her voice was no longer asking. "I'm coming."

Barbara remained silent as a battle for what her body craved and what her head argued against was being fought. "No, Taya."

Gently Barbara put down the receiver. She closed her eyes and breathed deeply.

It had to end, she told herself.

Barbara was shaken out of her thoughts as the phone began ringing again.

"I said no," she said immediately into the phone.

"No to what, Barbara?" Dale said from the other end.

Shit! Barbara thought. "It was a sales call, Dale. Sorry."

At that moment the doorbell rang.

"Dale, someone's at the door. I gotta go." She didn't want to do battle with her sister right now. She was tired of avoiding questions right and left from Dale.

"Yeah, it's Mom," Dale added guiltily.

Chapter Thirteen

"Taya, the candy will be on the street tomorrow."

"Why tomorrow? Why not tonight, Stanley?" Taya asked irritably.

"We haven't finished bagging it yet, Taya."

"Every minute the shit is not on the street we lose money, Stanley. What the fuck is taking so long? Fucking shit, Stanley! If you can handle this just tell me!"

"Taya, man, calm down. We have to take our time and weigh it." Stanley had been dealing with her foul mood for days now.

Taya looked like she was going to throttle him.

"I wanna make sure it's done right, Taya. If we get sloppy we start to mess up."

Stanley immediately realized the error of what he had said.

"You pretend to show me how to run my business?"

"Fuck no! Nobody can or will ever run the pens like you. You got a monkey on your back, Taya. Just cut it off." Stanley tried to reason with her and to his surprise she seemed to rein in her anger.

"No later than tomorrow, Stanley," she said as she walked out.

"Fuck..." Stanley thought he was going to piss his pants. "Fuck."

✝

Taya got on her bike and she sat for a moment.

Cut the monkey off your back, Stanley had said. Taya kicked the bike into life and rode toward nowhere. Nowhere always took her to what she knew, the street. What had she thought? This was her life—the pens, the games, the white, and the whores. This was her world and she liked it. Here she was Black Angel and she was beholden to no one. She had all she needed. She had all she wanted. And if she didn't have it all, all she had to do was take it.

She pulled up to one of Christopher's corners. Taya saw Belinda and called her over. Belinda walked toward the Black Angel with both anticipation and fear. Taya was here and she was calling for her.

"Want some company?" Belinda asked her with a smile.

"That depends," Taya said as she stared hungrily at the barely covered breasts in front of her. "I wanna work off some anger. You up for it?"

"I can do that."

"Get on."

†

"You want a drink?"

Belinda was surprised with the question.

"Sure, thanks."

Taya went to the cupboard and pulled out a bottle and two glasses. She poured two tumblers full of scotch, taking one glass and sitting down, placing the bottle on the floor next to her. Belinda took the glass of scotch Taya had left for her on the table not knowing quite what to expect. Taya had said she wanted to work out some anger. That in her trade could mean anything. But, Black Angel was not known to hurt the women in her bed too badly, not like the johns did.

With the johns, that meant a lot of pain and perhaps accidental death. Black Angel liked her sex rough but had never hurt a woman so bad that she couldn't get over it in a few days. So why not? Why not please Black Angel? She had chosen her above the others and the others knew it. Belinda smiled to herself.

Taya emptied her glass, reached for the bottle and filled it again and again with the amber-colored liquid. Belinda watched and waited. She had not known what to expect and now she guessed she was seeing a side of Black Angel that few got to see. Belinda clearly saw the frustration of indecision written on the woman's face. Taya's facial expression would go from pure anger to a sadness that could touch the soul. She stared at the mystery that was Black Angel; the woman in front of her was not only beautiful but, for a while, had held her fascination. Taya was something unpredictable and that in the pens meant survival. And now Belinda was seeing yet another layer. It would seem that all she was expected to do was just to be there and that pleased her. Taya had picked her, not one of the others but her. Surely, that meant something.

Belinda saw Taya staring at her as if she was somehow surprised to find her there.

"Is that your real hair color?"

"Yes," Belinda said and smiled. She waited for another question but it never came.

✝

Taya filled her glass yet again. She had lost count of how many times she had refilled the glass. Taya's head fell back and she moaned. The pain was still there. When would the alcohol just numb her senses so she would feel nothing inside? She kept drinking.

96

An hour later, Taya's head fell forward as the empty glass fell from her hand. It had gotten completely dark outside; the only light in the apartment filtered in from some streetlights that still worked out on the deserted street.

Belinda got up and walked over to her. She picked up the glass and put it on the table, then stood in front of Taya, not exactly sure what to do next. This was Black Angel in front of her. Her hand lightly caressed the dark head of hair that was in front of her. Black Angel's hair was thick and soft. How would it feel to caress her body? To touch her? To be wanted by her? There must be so much passion locked up behind such a sharp mind.

Taya looked up unexpectedly. Her vision was blurry and her speech was slurred.

"Barbara?" Taya said as she reached out desperately for Belinda.

Taya stood up on wobbly legs. Belinda took her into her arms, holding her up, then walked her toward the bedroom.

"Come on. I'm putting you to bed."

Taya became very complacent as she leaned against her. She lay down on the bed with no objection. Belinda was about to walk away when Taya's hand on her arm held her in place.

"Stay with me, Barbara," Taya pleaded.

Belinda had thought that when Taya called her Barbara earlier that it had been a mistake, like it didn't matter who she was. She now realized Taya actually thought she was Barbara, whomever Barbara was.

"Stay with me, Barbara, please," Taya pleaded again. There was so much emotion in that plea that Belinda hesitated for a moment then lay down. Taya's arms immediately surrounded her and pulled her close, her hands caressed her body softly as she held her tightly to her.

"I love you, Barbara," Taya whispered softly as she buried her face in Belinda's hair. "I love you."

Belinda held her breath for a moment before her arms held Taya as well. After a few minutes she heard Taya's steady breathing. Taya was asleep. Who was Barbara? Belinda closed her eyes and gave herself to being Barbara. If only for a few hours she wanted to be held by Taya. Never had she felt so safe nor so firmly held in love's embrace. She wanted to be Black Angel's Barbara if only for a little while.

✝

Taya woke up with a hell of a headache. "Oh God," she moaned as she tried opening her eyes. She opened one eye at a time, slowly, and then tried getting up. As she did, Taya realized she was not alone. She stared at Belinda as she stirred. Taya was trying to remember just how she had gotten there.

"Good morning," Belinda said sleepily.

Taya said nothing as she got up and went straight to the bathroom.

Belinda followed Taya hungrily with her eyes. She quickly noted that the softness from the woman who had held her through the night was gone, but the memory lingered.

Taya walked into the kitchen half an hour later. She froze for a moment as she saw Belinda's back to her.

Belinda turned around in time to see disappointment in those dark eyes before it was quickly hidden with Taya's usual look of sarcasm.

"You don't believe in food do you?" Belinda said quickly.

Taya walked past her and got a diet Coke out of the refrigerator, opened it and took a long swig.

"Why are you still here? You don't expect payment do you?" Taya said with disgust.

Belinda stared at her.

"What?"

"Hard to believe you are the same woman," Belinda said cryptically.

"What the hell are you talking about?" Taya sounded angry and her headache was getting worse by the second.

"You were so loving."

"What shit are you on, lady? I can't remember what happened last night but I can tell you it wasn't love!"

"Yes, yes it was."

Taya had a smirk on her face as she drank the rest of her Coke.

"Get out. I have a headache." She opened a drawer and pulled out a pack of cigarettes. She lit one and took a deep drag.

"Who is Barbara?"

Taya's hand stopped midway to her mouth. She visibly paled. Slowly she put out the cigarette that she had only taken a few puffs from.

"Don't know any Barbara. Now go, I'm tired."

"You said, 'I love you, Barbara.'" Belinda saw Taya pale some more.

"If me saying, I love you, Barbara, makes you feel better about last night, fine…now just get out…I have a fucking headache the size of Montana." Taya walked over to the refrigerator and took out another diet Coke.

"We didn't do anything last night. You thought I was Barbara and begged me to stay with you," Belinda said as she looked toward Taya for any sort of reaction. "You held me close and caressed me and said you loved me."

Taya closed her eyes and held them shut for only a moment. She remained silent.

"I loved somebody once too, Taya. She wasn't strong enough. When the time came she just…well…" Belinda's eyes filled with tears as the memory still hurt.

Taya looked toward her now and said nothing, but for a brief moment she saw the pain and shared it.

"I'm sorry, Belinda, but there is no Barbara," Taya said softly, but unable to hide the sadness of the statement.

"My Barbara's name was Laura," Belinda said sadly.

"My sister's name was Laura," Taya said softly, reminiscing. She walked over to the window and looked out at the street, lost in memories.

Belinda watched her for a few moments then decided it was best to leave Taya to sort out her thoughts. "Later, Black Angel. By the way, I didn't hear a thing," Belinda said as she left.

When Taya heard the door shut she allowed the tears to run down her face as she leaned her forehead against the glass. Why now? Why now when there was nothing left of her. Why now? she kept asking herself over and over again.

Chapter Fourteen

"Okay, what is going on with you?"

Barbara dropped the cup in the sink and turned around quickly.

"Jesus, Dale! You scared me to death. I want my key back if you insist on giving me a heart attack every other week." Barbara had her hand on her chest trying to catch her breath.

"I'm sorry I scared you. But, you have been processing long enough. Spill!"

"Do you want some coffee?" Barbara asked as she turned around to give herself some more time.

"Sure, why not. Now talk." Dale sat on the stool that she pulled out from under the island in the kitchen. She crossed her hands in front of her and waited for Barbara to speak. She was going to get some answers today if it killed both of them. Enough was enough.

Barbara prepared the coffeemaker and turned it on. She then turned toward her sister who seemed determined to extract the answers to her questions.

"I don't know what you expect me to say, Dale."

There was a moment of uncomfortable silence between them.

"Okay, normal stuff. Rob is playing golf today. I don't know why he loves that game so much. I find it so boring. Then there is Brian; I just dropped him off at school. God! That boy is going to make me old before my time. Mom wants me to get the recipe to those little hors d'oeuvres you made last Christmas. You know the ones with the dates. Then there is Ruffus; I need to take him to the veterinarian for his rabies shot."

Barbara stared at her as if she had lost her mind. Dale looked back at her sister and took a deep breath before speaking again.

"You know, Barb, when you were six Dad had some very important clients over for dinner." Dale saw Barbara smile. "Somehow a frog jumped on the dinner table and on top of the main course; the guy's wife just about passed out and the sauce splattered on Dad's client's shirt. Dad was furious and Mom was livid."

Dale smiled slightly and a giggle escaped her.

"I knew you did it, Barb. You can fool everyone on this planet but not me, little sister."

"You knew it was me?" Barbara laughed a little. "It was an accident really. It got away." They both laughed now.

"I thought that guy was going to bust a gut," Dale said as she laughed heartily.

"His wife fell off the chair." Barbara was bent over with laughter.

"Oh, Jesus, that was funny."

"I thought Dad was going to kill somebody," Barbara said as she began to breathe steadily, trying to control the laughter.

"Yeah."

Both women laughed some more as they drank coffee together. It was good to act like they used to. Dale had always been more than her sister. Dale had been her co-conspirator and her friend as they had grown up.

Barbara was smiling to herself when she was taken off guard by Dale's question.

"Why the sadness, Barbara?" Dale asked her with so much concern that she could not ignore it.

Barbara looked at her sister and then down at her cup of coffee.

"I want something I can't have." There, she'd said it. If she didn't talk about it at least a little she thought she would die.

Dale put her hand over her sister's.

"Is it Jeff?" Dale asked sympathetically.

"No," Barbara answered. Her eyes filled with tears and she looked down at her coffee cup again.

"We have always been able to talk to each other. I'm here, kid."

"Dale, I…I love someone that I can't…" Barbara became silent as the tears ran down her face.

"You love?"

"Oh, Dale, I never planned it. It just happened. Before I knew it…no, from the very first moment." Barbara covered her face with her hands.

Dale was silent. She wasn't exactly sure what to say. She had thought it had to do with Jeff, then as time passed she wasn't exactly sure and now…she wasn't sure of anything.

"Well, sweetheart, being in love doesn't have to be a bad thing. Not everyone is Jeff, you know. There are some really nice guys out there, Barb."

Barbara looked at her sister again and at that moment realized Dale would not understand. Some guy she had said…that's how people would always figure it was…some guy.

Barbara wiped her face. "No, it's over."

"Are you sure?"

"Yes."

"I'm sorry, Barbara," Dale said sadly. She tried changing the topic, thinking it might help. "How is your therapy going?"

Barbara stared at her for a moment then it clicked. "Oh, I, um, I stopped going."

"Why? I thought you…"

"No, it really wasn't helping you know." Barbara got up and started putting the breakfast dishes away.

"How is your friend Taya?"

"Taya?"

"Yeah, your biker pal." Dale smiled.

"Oh, Taya…I haven't seen her for a while."

"Barbara?"

"Yeah?" Barbara looked up at her sister now.

"This is the one you stayed that night with, isn't it?"

"Yes." Barbara was tired of the lies. She might not clear up everything but at least allowing herself to share some of her pain about Taya helped.

"This man you love. Are you sure it's over?"

Barbara looked down. "It's over. It never had a chance. We come from two totally different worlds. I just didn't want to see it."

†

"Jerry, have you seen Eric?" Barbara asked one of Eric's friends.

"No."

"If you see him will you tell him I'm here?"

"Sure."

Barbara had gotten to the school about five minutes later than usual and Eric was not where she normally picked him up. She got out of her car and waited a little longer. As usual,

Sean came trudging along a few minutes later with his buddies.

"Sean, have you seen Eric?"

"Nope."

"Mrs. Williams!"

Barbara looked toward Mrs. Bradford, the school principal.

"Yes?"

"Mrs. Williams, please come with me."

"What's wrong?"

"I've called the police."

Minutes later, Barbara sat in the principal's office in shock at the news Mrs. Bradford had relayed. She told Barbara that a student had run into her office and told her he had seen a green van pull up, take a boy and then quickly take off. The boy that had been taken was Eric Williams. She had called the police immediately and then went out to see if she could find Barbara. Sean looked at his mother with tear-filled eyes, seeking a reassurance she was unable to give him. So he sat patiently with her and held onto her hand tightly.

Mrs. Bradford walked back into the office.

"Can I get you something, Mrs. Williams?" the woman asked softly.

Barbara did not answer; she stared straight ahead, lost in her worry and fears. Sean looked at his mother and began to sob.

Barbara looked at her son then took him into her arms as the tears ran down her own face. "It's going to be all right, Sean. It's going to be all right."

Karen Bradford tried to keep from crying as her own eyes filled with tears. These things happened in other schools; never in her imagination did she ever think it would happen in hers.

She sat down next to Barbara and put her arms around her. How could this happen? She knew Eric Williams. He was a gentle boy, well liked by his teachers. How could something like this happen? she asked herself yet again. The hardest thing she had ever done in her life was to tell this woman that her child had been taken.

†

The police arrived and asked many questions then told Barbara to go home, that they would start looking for the van and would be in touch when they knew something.

Barbara stared at them in disbelief. "You will get in touch with me? When? Is that all? I want my son back!" Barbara was becoming hysterical.

"Mrs. Williams, we will do our best," the officer said, trying to be as understanding as possible.

"Let me drive you home," Mrs. Bradford volunteered.

"Thank you, but no, I will drive myself," Barbara blurted out. She was angry. Karen Bradford understood the frustration and remained silent. How could this poor woman not be upset?

"Mom?" Sean's hand filled hers.

"It's going to be okay, Sean," Barbara said, kneeling down in front of her son. She began to sob as she held him tightly to her.

In the end Mrs. Bradford called Barbara's sister, Dale. She and her husband had come by and taken Barbara and Sean home. The police put out an APB for the green van and started making inquiries. There wasn't much else they could do. They had asked for a recent photo of Eric, which they picked up a few hours later from the house.

†

The phone rang and Barbara ran to grab it.

"Hello?"

"Barbara?"

Barbara closed her eyes as tears ran down her face. "Taya, someone took Eric. Someone took my baby, Taya." Barbara began to sob as she held the phone tightly to her ear.

"Who took him?" Taya asked quickly.

"They don't know. They took my baby, Taya. They took him." Barbara couldn't speak anymore as the sobs became uncontrollable.

"I'll be right there, baby. We'll get him back. You'll see, we'll get him back." Taya felt as though her chest was being squeezed so hard she could hardly breathe. She hung up and ran down the stairs. All people saw was a Black Angel flying out of the pens.

Taya flew through the streets as a million horrible scenarios went through her mind. She shook her head. She refused to believe that anything she had thought of would apply to Eric. Not him. Not that boy. Not that special, beautiful boy.

Taya pulled up the driveway and jumped off her bike. She ran up the steps and walked in without knocking. Dale was sitting next to Barbara on the couch, holding her. A man she didn't know stood sadly by the wall. As soon as Barbara saw her she got up and ran straight into Taya's arms. Taya held her tightly to her.

"They took my baby. Oh God, they took my baby," Barbara sobbed.

"Barbara, we'll get him back." Taya held her as tears ran down her own face. She kissed Barbara's face and her lips. She looked into her eyes. "We will get him back," Taya stated with no doubt in her vow.

Barbara buried her face in Taya's neck and continued to weep. Dale stood up to rush to Barbara's side, but her husband walked over to her and held her in place. Dale looked at him as things suddenly began to get clearer.

"Do you have a recent picture of Eric you can give me?" Taya said as she pulled out of Barbara's arms.

"I already gave it to the police," Barbara said pitifully. All she wanted was for Taya to hold her. She felt that something inside her was dying and she couldn't bear to think too hard about anything.

"Do you have another?" Taya insisted.

"I can get you one," Dale said as she ran out of the room.

Barbara went back into Taya's arms. Taya stroked her hair and kissed her head and face again and again. "We will get him back, baby, we will get him back."

Dale came back into the room and Taya pushed Barbara away again as she took the photo and looked at it and smiled sadly.

"I'll be back," Taya said as she rushed out the door.

Barbara stared after her. "Taya…"

†

Taya was back within the hour but had not been any help at all, according to Dale. It seemed that Taya was outside on the veranda on the phone most of the time instead of where Barbara wanted her to be. There was something obviously going on between them, Dale thought. As to the extent Dale was not sure yet.

Joan Barrett had been notified and had not taken the news well. She was a mess. Sean was upstairs with his cousin, playing a game and that was good.

Taya came inside. "Where is Sean, Dale?"

"He's upstairs with Brian."

Taya walked up the stairs. Dale noted that she seemed to know where she was going. It would seem Taya knew the house quite well.

Taya stood by the door and watched Sean go through the motions of playing the video game. She knew too well how people detached themselves from feeling not to recognize the signs.

"Hi, squirt," Taya said softly.

Sean looked up and stared at her for a moment. She gave him a smile and he ran into her arms.

He tried to stifle a sob but did not quite succeed. He clung to Taya's waist and she knelt down in front of him and pulled him tightly against her.

"It's going to be okay, squirt. It's going to be okay." She wiped the tears away from his face and smiled. She caressed his head and took him into her arms again.

Barbara was only a few feet away and walked over to where they stood. Sean looked up and smiled bravely at his mother. Barbara could not control the tears as they ran down her face again.

Taya stood and lifted the boy up with her in her arms then pulled Barbara into the embrace as well.

A few minutes later Taya walked Barbara downstairs again. They sat down together with Barbara half lying on the sofa and half on Taya, who held her tightly and kept comforting her with caresses. Dale could not hear what she was saying but could only imagine. All that mattered right now, she kept telling herself, is that Barbara was holding up better with Taya by her side.

Taya's phone started ringing and again she left the room and went to speak on it outside. Barbara seemed to shrivel up into a little ball on the sofa and began to cry again.

Almost an hour later Taya was still outside on the phone and Dale was getting madder and madder. Barbara kept asking for her, so Dale went out to the deck to get her.

Dale stopped as soon as she heard Taya almost yelling into the cell phone.

"Rico, I need this favor!" Dale heard Taya say. She waited in the shadows. It had gotten dark and Eric had been missing for over eight hours.

"I'm looking for a boy… He was taken from a schoolyard… Rico, I am willing to pay whatever you want… No! Not tomorrow, Rico, now! You know that time is of the essence… He's my boy, Rico. He's my boy." Taya began to cry.

Dale listened and tried to understand what was going on.

"Yes… Rico, I will give you wh— yes, did you get the photo? He was taken this afternoon from his school… Yes, it was a green van… I know you have people that cover that area. Did Stanley give you all the details?"

Dale listened and waited.

"I have everyone looking for him, Rico, but I want a bigger area covered. You know that people like this don't go far." Taya ran her fingers through her hair.

Dale went back inside the house. Barbara looked at Dale with tear-filled eyes. She looked awful.

"Taya is getting some people to look for Eric too," was all that Dale said as she sat next to her sister.

"I tried calling Jeff but he's out of town and left no forwarding number. Dale, I'm scared. I'm so scared they are going to hurt him."

"That is not going to happen, Barbara. We're going to get him back safe and sound," Dale said as she cried silently while holding on to her sister.

✝

110

Taya paced outside like a wild animal in captivity. She knew that the more time that passed the harder it would be to find him, if they were able to find him at all. The type of people who did this were at the bottom of the cesspool. She closed her eyes, trying to remind herself that her people would find him. They had to. She sat down and covered her face and wept. Why? Why? Taya heard a lamenting cry and realized it was her.

The world these animals crawled out of was the world she lived in. She prospered from the trade of the white and all the violence and degeneracy that it promoted. Her world had touched this boy, her boy. How could she live with that? How could she live with the thought that who and what she was had taken him? The darkness that she lived in had spread its mantle and touched the part that she had tried so hard not to allow into her heart. Inside Barbara was dying by the minute. Sean played upstairs for the sake of not thinking and…suddenly she knew. She wanted a life with Barbara. She would die to give her the happiness she had once seen in those beautiful blue eyes. She would get Eric back. She had to. She had to or she would die trying. If anything happened to that boy…she could not bear what would come after.

"Do you think we will get him back?"

Taya got up and turned away, she wiped her face as she faced Dale. "We have to."

Dale heard the doorbell and ran inside followed by Taya.

Barbara led a policeman into the room. "We put out an APB, Mrs. Williams, earlier today. We know that your son's picture is everywhere. You have a good network set up."

Barbara looked puzzled.

"We know that everyone is looking for your boy. My sources tell me that every element of this city is looking for him, ma'am. This is a good thing, Mrs. Williams. It more than doubles our chances." The officer tried to reassure her kindly.

"What do you mean by every element?"

"Your son's photograph is on every pole and there is a person on almost every street corner asking about him," the officer said incredulously.

Barbara leaned into Taya who had come up to stand beside her. "Thank you, officer."

"You're quite welcome, ma'am. We will be in touch if we hear anything at all."

Barbara turned around and buried herself in Taya's arms. At that moment Taya's cell phone rang. Taya let go of Barbara and walked outside again. Barbara stared at Taya as she walked away from her, wrapping her arms around her body in an effort to contain the pain and need.

Angry again, Dale went outside to Taya. She knew Taya was trying to help but she had to be a little bit more sensitive in how she treated Barbara.

Again Dale waited and listened.

"Stanley, don't do anything, you hear me! Send somebody in to make sure no harm comes to him and wait for me and Rico. Do you hear me, Stanley?" Taya was growling.

Dale stood behind her, waiting.

"I know where that is, I'll be there in fifteen minutes. Keep it under control, Stanley."

Taya turned to face Dale.

"Did you find him?" Dale could not believe or dared not hope that she had heard what she thought she had heard.

"I hope so. Don't say anything to Barbara." Taya tried to walk past Dale.

"Where? Tell me something, damn it!"

Taya grabbed Dale roughly by the arms. "I don't have time. Time is not on our side. Trust me. I want to get him back."

"Go," Dale said and Taya flew out of the house.

Barbara saw her leave and leaned into her brother-in-law who sat with her on the sofa. Dale looked at her husband and smiled a smile full of hope.

Chapter Fifteen

"Are you sure they have him, Stanley?"

"The new boy fits the description. And I looked in the garage. There's a green van inside. Rico's people found it an hour ago. Christopher is in there with one of his girls."

"I said one person, Stanley," Taya hissed.

"Yeah, you did. But we thought if things got out of hand Christopher could take care of things and someone could take care of the boy. So one of his girls said she would do it. You know the one." Stanley saw understanding register on Taya's face.

At that moment a black sedan pulled up and Rico got out. Within seconds, two unmarked patrol cars appeared as well.

"Ready to go in?" Rico asked Taya point-blank.

"Yeah."

"Here." One of the police officers handed them police-issued revolvers. Taya looked down and nodded in understanding. It was a tradeoff. She didn't care what it took; she wanted the boy back at any cost.

They stormed the house and shots rang out. Taya felt a slight discomfort to her side as she ran in but ignored it. She looked around and immediately saw Christopher holding a man against the wall.

"Is he the one?" she growled.

Christopher nodded. "This is the man of the hour."

"Where is my boy?" she asked him, controlling her desire to pound him through the wall. The man pinned against the wall spit into her face. She shot him in the kneecap and the guy cried out in pain.

"Where is my boy?" she growled as she put the gun to his head.

"The house is surrounded, Taya. No one is getting out of here." Rico was right behind her.

"Belinda is here somewhere. She was supposed to find him while I kept this piece of shit busy." Christopher pushed the guy harder against the wall.

"Where is he?" She cocked the gun against his head.

"In one of the rooms downstairs," he cried. He tried leaning down to grab his leg and she kicked where she had shot him.

"Ahh…" he screamed.

"If you lied to me I'm going to kill you. If you hurt him you will pray for death." Taya got really close to his face.

Taya ran down the stairs with Rico right behind her. Confronted with several doors she started opening them, finding empty rooms each time until she opened the last door. Taya's eyes searched the room and saw two shadows huddled in the corner. She flipped the light switch and saw Belinda holding a blond-haired child.

"Eric?" Taya said softly.

The boy looked up and ran into Taya's arms as she fell to her knees.

"Eric. Oh God, Eric." Taya held him tightly as tears ran down her face.

Rico took a few steps back and looked around to make sure there were no other surprises.

"Taya, I wanna go home," Eric said as he clung to her.

"I'm here to take you home, Eric. I'm going to take you back to your mama, my sweet, sweet boy." Taya wept as she kissed the blond head over and over.

Belinda sat in the corner, watching, then she smiled. Taya looked toward her, still holding tight to Eric and nodded her thanks.

"Barbara's boy?"

Taya nodded and got up still holding the boy tightly to her. "Let's go home, Eric."

He pulled away for a moment. "I remembered what you said."

"What was that?"

"You said if I was ever in trouble you would be there." He hid his tear-stained face in her neck again.

"Always and forever." Taya kissed the boy again and hugged him tightly to her. Keeping Eric well covered with her coat—he had seen enough…too much—she walked out of the room with Eric in her arms and Rico guarding her back.

Upstairs, Taya shot a look to Christopher who acknowledged both her thanks and her desire as to what was to be done with the kidnapper with a slight tip of his head.

Stanley opened the door to one of the black sedans that waited outside and she climbed into the backseat with Eric in her arms. Stanley slid behind the wheel and Rico got in next to him. They pulled out, escorted by the other two sedans and two marked police cars.

Eric began to cry and Taya held him tighter. "Shhh…it's okay, Eric. It's okay we're going home." She consoled him as he wept and cried silently herself as she caressed him and kissed him again and again.

Rico looked at Stanley. "Do your people know what must be done?"

"Perfectly," Stanley answered without any hesitation.

Chapter Sixteen

Dale watched two police cars and three black sedans pull into the driveway. Holding her breath in fear, she left the window and went to stand next to Barbara as Rob opened the front door.

Barbara looked toward the door and could not believe what she was seeing. Taya walked in with Eric in her arms. Barbara broke free from Dale and ran to take her son into her arms. "Thank God, Eric. Oh thank God!" she sobbed.

Eric cried as he clung to her.

Taya knew no matter what happened after this moment, or what it would cost her, it would all be worth it.

Two policemen then walked in with several other men and explained that the house had been raided and the men who had taken Eric had been shot during the raid.

"We are just glad that this had a happy ending, Mrs. Williams," one of the officers said as he was leaving.

Dale noticed Taya walk outside with the plainclothes officers and followed her. She knew Taya had something to do with how Eric was rescued and for Barbara's sake she had to find out what her role was.

When she saw Taya talking to one of the men she listened. She had to keep her sister safe. She just knew that something about this whole thing did not add up.

"Stanley…" Taya extended her hand and he took it. "Thank you." He nodded and smiled as he walked off with four other men. She then turned toward the man next to her.

"Thank you, Rico," Taya said as she shook the man's hand.

"Hey, the cops looked good and we got the boy back." Rico laughed. "Gotta feed the cops occasionally."

"I will keep my word. Whatever you want, name it. I will always be in your debt," Taya said with feeling.

"There is no debt, Taya. I have two of my own, a boy and a girl." Rico smiled.

Taya nodded in understanding.

"*Tu mujer?*" Rico nodded toward the house asking but already knowing the answer to the question he asked.

"*Sí.*" Taya confirmed that Barbara was her woman then once again took his hand. "I'm in your debt for life, Rico, for life."

"This wasn't business, Taya, this was family. No debt incurred. Hey, *consorte*, take care of that scratch. She's very lovely." Rico smiled boyishly.

Taya nodded her thanks and with that Rico walked away and left her staring after him as he did.

Taya watched as the cars pulled away. She then turned to go inside the house and saw Dale standing in the shadows.

Neither woman said a thing as both walked inside together.

Chapter Seventeen

Barbara had taken Eric into the family room after the police left. Sean had gone with her and now both boys were asleep in her arms. Taya smiled and leaned against the wall as she beheld the three on the sofa. After a while Barbara went upstairs to put Eric and Sean to bed. Dale and her husband were about to leave when Taya made an unusual request.

"Dale, can you stay for a bit longer?"

Dale seemed surprised. "Sure," she said and turned to her husband. "Sweetheart, why don't you go home with Brian. Mom is there and she will feel better if you are in the house. I'll stay here tonight."

"Sure, I understand. I'll come by to pick you up tomorrow okay?"

"Perfect."

After Dale had said her goodbyes to Rob and Brian, she went looking for Taya. She had seen Taya walk into one of the bathrooms downstairs and now stopped outside the door.

"Is that you, Dale?"

"Yes."

"Come in."

Dale blinked once or twice with surprise then walked into the bathroom.

"Close the door," Taya said.

Dale inhaled in surprise as she saw blood on the sink then quickly looked toward Taya.

"I need you to help me. I can't take off this damn coat," Taya said in exasperation. Suddenly Dale saw the blood on Taya's clothing.

"We have to take you to the hospital," Dale said immediately.

"No hospital. Will you help?" Taya waited for her response.

Dale looked at Taya for a moment then nodded her head.

"This happened when you went to get Eric?"

Taya nodded. Dale gently helped her take off the coat and saw that the inside lining of the coat was covered in blood as well.

Taya sat on the toilet and leaned her head back for a moment, trying to catch her breath. She took a deep breath and sat up straight. "Okay, help me to take off my T-shirt."

Dale could see the pain that it might cause to lift the T-shirt over her head so she looked in the cabinet under the sink for scissors to cut the T-shirt off instead. Taya now sat in front of her topless and covered in blood.

"Jesus, Taya, looks like you've lost a lot of blood." Then Dale saw the wound. It was on her side and it was bleeding profusely. "We have to get you to a doctor, Taya."

"Not a good idea," Taya said as she leaned her head against the wall to the side.

Dale looked at her then started digging around in the medicine cabinet. She found the antiseptic and some bandages. She saw that there were actually two wounds as she began to clean away the blood.

The bathroom door suddenly flew open and Barbara stood frozen to the spot. She seemed to stand straighter as she looked deeply into Taya's eyes, which were staring back at her.

"I'll take care of this, Dale." Barbara took the cloth that Dale was holding. "Can you please check on the boys?"

"Sure," Dale said and left.

Barbara got some other things out of the bottom drawer under the sink and began to clean out Taya's wound. A bullet had apparently gone through her side and had clearly gone out the other end. She was bleeding but it had slowed down some after Barbara applied some pressure.

"You brought Eric back," Barbara stated, she did not ask. She looked up to meet Taya's eyes. "Thank you for bring my baby back to me."

Taya said nothing.

Barbara continued to clean the wound and spread the antibacterial ointment on thickly before she taped the bandages. "You're going to need to see someone. I have some antibiotics upstairs. You will start to take those. But, you are going to have to see a doctor to make sure there is no infection."

"Barbara, I can't…"

"Not right now…but if necessary, you must." Barbara did not look like she was going to accept any argument.

Taya nodded and bent her head. She was tired and beginning to feel dizzy.

Barbara lifted Taya's face up with her index finger. Taya looked pale. She looked deeply, with concern, into the dark eyes that held her heart. "Taya…"

"You don't owe me anything, Barbara," Taya said suddenly.

"I will always be grateful for my son, Taya," Barbara said immediately.

"I don't want your gratitude," Taya replied angrily. She tried to get up and sat back down quickly. The pain seared through her, showing in her face.

"Sit down! Before you make it worse," Barbara scolded.

Taya sat but looked away.

"If you don't want my gratitude what do you want?" Barbara was surprised when those dark eyes turned to her then looked away quickly.

"Do you want me, Taya?" Barbara asked softly.

In pain Taya closed her eyes for a moment then opened them again. "As I said, you don't owe me anything."

"There is nothing I can give you?" Barbara asked softly, longing to hold her and never let her go.

"No, I don't want anything." Taya bent her head again. She squeezed her eyes shut. She didn't want gratitude. She had to go. She had to run and never look back.

"Not even my love, Taya?"

Taya looked up suddenly, and stood up quickly. The pain didn't matter. Her muscles were sore, the adrenaline rush had passed…but who cared.

"Don't play with me, Barbara," Taya growled as she grabbed Barbara by both arms. "Not about this."

"How could I not love you? From the very first moment you became my knight in shining armor. I love you, Taya," Barbara said. She tried to kiss Taya but Taya pulled away from her.

"I am no knight in shining armor! Don't lie to yourself about me. I am… Barbara, I am the kind of person someone like you crosses the street to avoid." Taya tried to keep Barbara at arm's length.

It was better this way, Taya told herself. To hold her now and then to have to let her go later would be more pain than she thought she could bear.

"I don't care what you've done or who you have been! I don't care! You saved Eric. You saved me," Barbara insisted. "I know who you are…I see it in your eyes when I look at you."

"I…I got him back because I thought I owed you." Taya tried anything to push Barbara away at this point. It would be so easy to take Barbara in her arms and say the words. But, it wouldn't be fair to Barbara. Taya tried walking past her.

"Owed me?" Barbara held her in place.

"For…" Taya could not bring herself to say it.

"For?"

"Oh Jesus, Barbara. I fucked you, okay. I liked it. I did this to…" Taya blurted out desperately.

"Liar," Barbara said softly.

"Barbara, I am not…"

Barbara kissed her tenderly and all Taya could do was cling to her for dear life. All of her resolve disappeared in the power of that one kiss.

"Liar," Barbara said again as she caressed the face of the woman in front of her.

"I'm no good, Barbara." Taya avoided her eyes, fighting the desire to kiss those lips again.

"Look at me and tell me you feel nothing for me."

Taya looked into the clearest blue eyes she had ever seen. "How could I not love you? Damn it!" Taya took her into her arms and held her tightly. "I'm not good for you, Barbara." Taya wept.

"It's going to be all right. We will make it all right." Barbara held her. Taya seemed so frail at that moment.

"I love you, Barbara. I didn't want to…but, God forgive me, I do. I love you so much it hurts. I can't stand being away from you anymore. When you told me about Eric, I knew. I couldn't deny it to myself anymore. It became so clear. I couldn't breathe. He is so much like you. He and Sean. I look at them and my heart aches. I…"

"It's going to be okay, my love. We are going to make it okay, I believe that." Barbara held Taya and for once Taya allowed someone to console her.

"Oh God, Barbara, I love you. All I know is that I love you." Taya said in desperation. She knew it could never last.

She knew it would end, but for one moment she needed to believe it would last forever. Taya gave herself to the mirage.

†

Dale leaned on the wall outside the bathroom. She had heard most of the conversation. Finally, all the pieces fit. When had the world turned upside down? she asked herself.

Dale walked away leaving Barbara and Taya to the rest of their conversation in private.

My sister? Dale thought as she walked in a daze. Why is it such a shock? I knew what that guy Rico had asked Taya. I know enough Spanish to know he was asking Taya if Barbara was her…Jesus!

Dale sat down on the sofa in the family room.

Barbara and Taya are…Jesus! So many things made sense now. Was Taya the impossible relationship? Of course she was. It all added up. No wonder Barbara felt so isolated and confused. Then again, who would have suspected.

Dale shook her head. So many questions and no answers, not really. The one thing that was a fact was that Taya had been instrumental in getting Eric back. She knew for a fact that without Taya they might not have ever gotten him back and for that, if nothing else, she owed Taya the benefit of the doubt. Taya had saved Eric from…she didn't even want to think what might have happened to him. And Taya had saved Barbara…yes, Taya had saved Barbara from one thing, but had it only been to get her into something even more frightening?

The truth was that Taya came from a place she didn't want Barbara to be a part of. Dale could tell that Taya's words of love seemed to be honest but…

Dale got up and headed back to the two women. The questions would have to answer themselves in time. The choices in the end were not hers to make. She would wait and see.

✝

"Here, let's put this around you until we get you upstairs," Barbara said as she gently wrapped a towel around Taya's naked torso.

"Barbara, I shouldn't stay."

"Don't even say another word! Do you hear me?"

Taya was about to say something when she saw Dale appear at the door.

"Barbara…" Dale said softly. "Maybe, you should let her go."

Barbara stared at her sister with disbelief. "She is going nowhere but upstairs to bed. She's hurt and she's stubborn and SHE," Barbara turned toward Taya, "will do as I SAY." Barbara's words left no room for argument.

Barbara helped Taya up the stairs as Dale followed closely behind. Barbara took her into her bedroom. She was beyond caring what Dale thought at this point. In the last twenty-four hours she thought she had lost her son, and Taya had brought him back to her. Taya was hurt and nothing anyone said or thought mattered. She had Eric back and she had Taya. Her boys were both safe, all she loved she wanted close to her for one night. If only for one night, she needed that.

Taya sat down on the bed looking very pale and exhausted. Barbara pulled the covers back and helped her lay down. Taya closed her eyes for a moment as exhaustion overtook her. Barbara started pulling Taya's pants off when she realized Dale was next to her, helping her undress Taya. Barbara covered Taya and went into the bathroom.

125

Taya closed her eyes as she let out her breath slowly. She had not realized just how tightly wound she had been until that moment.

"Mommy!"

Taya sat up quickly and grabbed her side as pain rocketed through her. The sound of glass breaking came from the bathroom and Barbara ran out soon after.

"Dale…"

"Go, I'll stay with her."

Barbara ran out of the room as Dale stopped Taya from getting out of bed. She pushed her back on the bed softly but firmly.

"Listen, you just relax, superwoman," Dale said with a touch of humor.

"I want to go and see…" Taya fell back on the bed. She began to visibly perspire as she felt nausea overtaking her.

"Hey, Taya, you look as white as a ghost." Dale looked down and saw a red stain growing on the white sheet that was covering Taya. "Shit, you are bleeding through the sheet. You need a doctor." Dale got up but Taya grabbed her arm and held her in place.

"No, I'll go," Taya said as she got up. She was holding on to Dale's arm still. "I don't want to pull Barbara into this. I'll go, okay. It will be better this way anyway. You agree with me, don't you?" Taya knew the answer without having to hear it.

Dale stood motionless as Taya grabbed for her clothes while holding her side all the while.

Taya was in pain, and if she was honest with herself she wasn't sure how far she would get. She knew at this point that she needed to see somebody but going to the hospital would mean questions. Questions that she couldn't answer and questions that might bring her more trouble later. She knew somebody who could help her but she couldn't have him come to Barbara's home. She refused to allow her world to come here. She was willing to die if necessary.

"What do you think you're doing?" Barbara asked from the door. "Dale, why did you let her get up?"

Taya stood naked in front of her, clutching her clothes to her. "Barbara, it's better this way," was all she said as Barbara walked over to her.

"For who?"

"For you. It's better for you," Taya said as a tear ran down her cheek. Taya was tired of fighting the world, tired of fighting her feelings for Barbara and fighting herself.

Placing her hand behind Taya's head Barbara pulled her mouth to hers. She kissed her soundly with all the love she felt for her. Dale stood stock-still not wanting to look, yet unable to look away.

"And now that that is taken care of, get back in that bed," Barbara said as she caressed Taya's face. "I am not ashamed of my love for you. I am not hiding."

Taya turned her head to look at Dale who suddenly found something interesting on the floor to look at.

"I'll call Jean. Ted, her husband, is a doctor."

"No."

"Yes. You are bleeding again and we need to have someone who knows what they are doing look at you."

"Barbara…"

"No hospital right?"

"No," Taya answered softly.

"Those policemen…" Barbara trailed off. "You know them…" Again Barbara got her answer from the silence.

Taya searched her eyes. Barbara had an idea of what she was but that idea was miles away from the reality, yet she was still there, still holding on, still loving her.

"Is there someone that we can call?" Barbara tried again.

"I don't want to bring anyone here, Barbara," Taya said as she grabbed Barbara for support.

Barbara immediately steadied Taya to keep her from falling. "Back to bed. I'll call Jean."

Taya was barely conscious as Barbara helped her back into bed.

"Stay with her, Dale. And this time don't let her get up."

†

"Well, she really should go to the hospital, Barbara," Ted said as he wrote on a prescription pad.

"I know, Ted, but she won't go."

Ted looked up for a moment then continued writing.

"She's in good health and fortunately the bullet went through mostly fatty tissue; it didn't come close to any vital organs. The stitches will help with the bleeding." He then handed Barbara several prescriptions. "Make sure she takes the antibiotics faithfully and the dressing should be changed often. She shouldn't get it wet. Follow the instructions I have written down. I'll come by tomorrow to check on her."

"Thank you, Ted," Barbara said appreciatively.

"You're welcome. I'm happy to help. I'm glad about your boy, Barbara. We all feel safer now that they got those people."

Barbara smiled as she walked Ted and Jean to the door.

"I'll take over the carpool till you have things under control, Barb. Don't worry about it okay?" Jean said as she hugged her friend.

"Thank you, Jean. I'll call you tomorrow."

After closing the door Barbara came face-to-face with Dale.

"I just checked on the boys again…they are both fast asleep." Dale ran her fingers through her hair. "Mom called."

"Did she?" Barbara felt the emotional drain of the ordeal hit her. "I'm going to the twenty-four-hour pharmacy on Elm Street. I'll be right back."

"No, I'll do it. You stay here. I think here is where you want to be…and I can do this for you," Dale said with a smile.

"Okay, thanks." Barbara handed Dale the prescriptions and kissed her sister on the cheek. "Thank you." Barbara hugged her sister tightly.

✝

I am lying upstairs in Barbara's house in Barbara's bed. That was the thought going through Taya's mind. How she had gotten here no longer mattered. Perhaps, fate had brought her this far so she could give Eric back to her. One thing was certain…for right now she was happy. She was grateful for the mercy she had received from a god she no longer believed in or prayed to.

Taya closed her eyes and remembered another time and another life when praying was as expected as breathing. She recalled all the details that had brought her to where she was now…how had it happened? She had always thought she was the strong one. She had not only survived, she ran the pens…she… Taya suddenly realized she was the one who had failed. She was the failure.

Her mother had tried to stop her. Her sister and her brother had tried too. All she heard was her own desire…her anger. Her anger had blinded her and brought her to this. She could blame her father, but then she realized that the only person to blame was herself.

How long would it be till Barbara saw what her mother had seen and throw her away too? One day Barbara would know the truth and it would all end. Taya looked around the room with longing. This is what she was not allowed to have. She was living on borrowed time. She had forfeited the right to this life long ago. In the end she realized there were no choices…she could no more leave what she was than Barbara could become a part of her life. No, she could not bring Barbara into her life. Her life was ugly and…Barbara deserved better. Barbara and her boys deserved much better.

Taya closed her eyes as tears escaped them. At least she had been there to save Eric…that was her only solace. She should leave, Taya told herself over and over again. But, how could she? How could she walk away from air to breathe or water to drink? Barbara had become necessary to living. Yet she knew that it could not last. It would exist for a little while, but the moment that it ended so would Taya.

"A life with you, *querida,* what I wouldn't I give for a life with you." Taya wept. "Just a little while, just a little longer, *querida.* Long enough to last me a lifetime," Taya whispered the secret to the empty room.

Taya saw the justice of it and smiled upward. "Thank you. Even a little while is more than I deserve."

†

Barbara checked on the boys and leaned down to kiss each one. She thanked God yet again for her miracles. She slowly walked to her bedroom. She closed the door behind her and her eyes immediately sought out Taya. Barbara smiled down tenderly at the sleeping woman then slid under the blanket and held the woman she loved and quietly wept. Taya had pulled her out of her impending death. Taya had gotten her child back. Barbara cried herself to sleep.

An hour later Dale poked her head in to make sure that they were all right. Before she closed the door Taya began to mumble in her sleep and Barbara caressed the face she dearly loved whispering reassurances in her ear. "No more nightmares, my darling, you're safely home. I love you, Taya. I love you. Tonight, I watch over you. Sleep well, my darling. Sleep well."

Dale watched them for a moment before she closed the door softly.

Chapter Eighteen

"Mamá, qué le pasó a Laura?" Taya knew that something awful had happened to her sister.

"Enrique abusó de ella." Her mother broke down in tears as she revealed how her eldest daughter had been raped by her boyfriend.

"No!" Taya went to run out the door as her mother tried to stop her.

"No! No Taya, no hagas una locura. La policía lo está buscando." Her mother tried to stop her to no avail. Taya was not about to let the police handle things. She would make her own justice.

"Ahhh!!!!" Taya screamed as she sat upright. She looked at herself, searching.

"Taya, what's wrong, darling? What's wrong?" Barbara sat up next to her in confusion.

"Blood, there's blood everywhere! Blood!" Taya shouted, disoriented.

Barbara quickly turned the light on, her eyes searching for signs of blood on Taya and saw nothing.

"Blood! I'm covered in blood!" Taya shouted as she tried to pull off the sheet that covered her.

Dale burst into the room gand stared at the half-crazed woman yelling.

"Taya! Taya, darling, there is no blood." Barbara held Taya's face, making her look at her. "There is no blood, darling. There is no blood."

Taya began to breathe easier and her eyes held Barbara's for dear life.

Dale stared in fear at both of them from the doorway.

"There is no blood, darling. You're safe. There is no blood. Now lie down and rest, Taya, rest," Barbara said softly as she pushed her down and kissed her lips lightly. Almost as soon as Taya's head hit the pillow her eyes closed and within seconds she was asleep.

"Jesus, what happened?" Dale asked quietly.

Barbara placed her finger to her lips to signal Dale not to speak. She then got up slowly and walked out of the room with Dale.

"What happened?"

"I'm not sure. I'm going to check on the boys." Barbara walked toward the boys' bedroom as Dale followed.

Barbara walked in quietly and sat on the edge of Eric's bed. She caressed his head as tears yet again slid down her face. She kissed him lovingly on the forehead and also kissed Sean before she left the room.

Dale followed Barbara downstairs. She went into the kitchen and turned the light on.

"Want some tea?"

"Yes." Dale sat down.

Barbara had kept herself sane the past twenty-four hours by being busy. It seemed the appropriate thing to do at the time as well.

"What happened?" Dale asked concern obvious on her face.

"I think she had a nightmare. It's no wonder. I don't even want to think about what she did to…"

Dale met Barbara's eyes and looked away again.

"She's a killer, Bar…"

"She saved my son!"

Dale looked down at her hands. "Yes, I know."

Barbara opened her mouth to speak then turned and started getting the cups ready instead.

"Don't you think I know what she is?" Barbara said with her back to Dale. "I don't care."

"Barbara…I'm glad she saved Eric too," Dale said softly.

"That's all that matters."

"Okay, we won't talk about it now," Dale said, accepting for the moment.

"No!" Barbara turned around suddenly and faced Dale, anger written clearly in her face. "We will not. Dale, no more questions. I won't allow any."

"But Barbara…"

"None, Dale. I love you but don't make me choose. I am hanging on to sanity here. I don't care. Do you understand me?" Barbara began to cry. "I don't care what she is or what she's done…" She covered her face and began sobbing.

Dale walked around and held onto her sister tightly. "It's all going to be okay, sis, it's going to be okay."

"I know what she is, Dale, she never lied to me. I can only imagine what happened tonight…those men…I don't care. She saved my baby. She saved my baby, Dale. She would have died for him. I know that." Barbara held on to Dale as she wept.

"I know, Barb. I know."

"I don't want to know anymore. I don't want to know anything." Barbara sobbed even harder. "Oh God, Dale…I'm afraid what she might tell me if I asked."

Dale held her sister tighter. "Okay, Barb. Okay." Dale began to cry as well.

"I love her, Dale. I love her."

✝

Barbara checked on both the boys and Taya all night. She just couldn't seem to rest without doing it over and over again. Dale finally made her lay down by promising that she would keep checking on them.

Barbara woke up on the sofa with a small warm bundle next to her. She recognized her son's head as she opened her eyes. "Sean? Are you all right, baby?"

"Just love you, Mom. We went into your room and didn't find you. Eric fell asleep with Taya."

"They are both in my room?"

"Yeah, he knew she was here he said. When he saw her in your bed he just lay next to her and fell asleep."

"Okay, sweetheart. Are you okay?" Barbara caressed her son's curly hair.

"I'm still scared inside. I was so scared, Mom." Sean began to cry as Barbara held him tighter to her.

"I know. I was too, sweetie. But now it's all good."

"I couldn't believe it when she brought him back. How did she find him, Mom? I thought we would never see him again."

"We were so lucky, Sean. We were so lucky that she did find him."

"Yeah."

Barbara left Sean in the kitchen with Dale, who promised to make him blueberry pancakes, so Barbara went upstairs to check on Eric and Taya. She walked into her bedroom quietly. The scene before her moved her heart beyond any emotion she had ever experienced.

Eric had his arms around Taya's neck and she in turn held him tightly to her. Tears ran down Barbara's face. It is said that children see things clearer than any adult could. At that moment Barbara saw it clearly. She walked to the bed and got in on the other side of Eric and lay down as well. Her arms went protectively over her son and she put her face on his head.

Chapter Nineteen

"Barbara? What's going on? I have at least five messages here from the police department about Eric being missing." Jeff's strident tone set Barbara on edge.

"He was taken from school a week ago, Jeff."

"How? If he is not going to be safe with you then I'm…"

"If he isn't going to be safe with me? Why you arrogant son of a bitch! I tried reaching you and you left no number! I didn't even know you were going away. He was abducted, Jeff! Just thank God that we got him back and he is alive." Barbara wept. "Think of someone else besides yourself."

"I want to see my son," he said indignantly.

"We have an appointment at three this afternoon with a doctor. You can come after we get back."

"I thought you said he was okay?"

"It's a therapist, Jeff. It was a very frightening experience for him. He needs to talk about it so that he feels better."

"Yes, that makes sense," Jeff said, realizing his ex-wife had good reason for her anger.

"I'll call you when we get back. Will you have your cell phone on?" Barbara tried to control her anger.

"Yes."

"Okay then."

"Barbara?"

"Yes," she said tiredly.

"I'm sorry."

"You're always sorry, Jeff. I tried to call you to tell you. You should have left a number or something. Something could happen to either of them and you would never have known."

There was a long silence.

"I know. I'm sorry, Barbara. For so much."

"All right. I'll call you when we get back so you can see him."

"Thanks. I'll be waiting. I love you all, you know."

"Oh God, Jeff, let's just deal with Eric okay? He needs to know that you are here for him too."

"Of course, Barbara. Call me when you get back."

Barbara hung up the phone. How could she ever have married someone as callous as Jeff?

She thought back over the past week and a smile covered her face. In spite of all the pain it was Taya who had brought the laughter, Taya who held Eric when he sought safety. He clung to her and she patiently reassured him over and over again. Her love was so evident in all her words and in the way she held him. She never tired of his questions or of his need.

It was Taya who encouraged Sean when he had come from school and admitted to her that he hated that he had to have special lessons to help him read. It was Taya who patiently reassured him that he would overcome this and would do well. It was also Taya who had somehow managed to have a series of books and videos delivered the next day with things that she knew Sean loved to encourage him to read. It had been the same Taya who had sat patiently with him and read to him and listened as he made the effort as well.

Taya had shown them more love and kindness in one week than Jeff had in their whole lives and she did it because she wanted to not because she had to.

Barbara could not and would not see anything beyond that. That other woman that lurked in the background could not be Taya. The woman that she first met was something else, someone else. She refused to believe they were one and the same. She had the proof in front of her, Taya laughing, Taya's eyes filled with love, Taya's hands that only gave love, Taya with the boys sitting on the floor in the other room laughing while they all played video games. This was her world and she would hang on to that.

✝

An hour later Taya was walking down the stairs.

"Where do you think you are going?" Barbara stepped out from the living room.

"I have some things I have to take care of."

"You know you shouldn't be out yet. I know you heal quickly and all," Barbara tried to keep it light, "but, you are not superwoman you know. Besides your wound might..."

Taya smiled and interrupted her. "You know you are a mother hen, but I am not one of your chicks. And yes, I am a fast healer. Now, I'll be back by tonight. I promise." Taya stopped right in front of her.

"Why can't you just stay here?" Barbara looked into her eyes imploringly. "Just stay here. You don't have to go back there."

Taya heard what she was asking quite clearly. Barbara's eyes no longer held the playfulness of the moment before. Her fear was quite visible now.

"I have to go. I just can't..."

"Why?" Barbara insisted, her hand grasping Taya's arm.

"Because it would all get out of control and…" Taya looked down at the hand holding her.

"And?"

"Don't ask me any more questions, Barbara." Taya's eyes now challenged her. "I can't answer them right now," Taya said coldly and tried pulling away.

"And if I ask you not to go?" Barbara tried again, still hanging on to Taya's arm.

"Don't ask me."

Barbara released her and turned her back to her. For a moment Taya almost took her into her arms. But she didn't. Taya knew that the streets were waiting. She had not been seen for a week and in the pens that meant only one thing…the cockroaches would start to come out.

"I have to go." Taya stopped and looked longingly at the back of her lover. "I'll come back…if you want me to," she added softly, trying to hide the fear in her voice.

Barbara turned around and went straight into her arms.

"I want you back. I will always want you back," she said as she clung to Taya tightly. "I love you, Taya." Barbara could not stop the tears from coming. "Please come back to me safely."

"Oh, Barbara. Please don't cry. I'll be back before you know it." Taya held her tighter still. "I promise."

Taya kissed her passionately then suddenly released her and went out the door.

Barbara wrapped her arms around her body and closed her eyes tightly as she wept.

†

She wasn't even close to one hundred percent but no one knew that. She had to show herself in the pens or she would be history and she knew it. The last thing she wanted or could handle right now was a power war.

So she was more visible than usual. Taya stopped at a couple of places where the white was made ready for the street and a few of the stables. The money was coming in and all were paid their shares. Her last stop was to see Belinda.

When she pulled up and Belinda saw her she knew that she had kept her secret.

"Hello, Dark Angel," Belinda said with a smile and loud enough for all to hear.

Taya nodded. "I wanted to…"

"It's okay," she said softly.

Taya immediately met her eyes. "You need anything?"

"I'm okay."

"If you ever do…"

"The only thing I want no one can give me." Belinda smiled sadly.

Taya looked around and remained quiet.

"Thanks," Taya said softly as she met her eyes again then cranked her bike and rode away.

"You're welcome," Belinda said to the wind and smiled.

"What did she want? God, she is gorgeous," a voice asked excitedly.

Belinda turned around and faced a young woman new to the stables. Belinda smiled. "She is that, and what she wanted I am the only one that gives her, understand?" Belinda played it to the hilt.

"Hey! All right, B, no problems." The girl took a step back. "I would never play you. You've been good to me."

"You remember that, little girl. The only thing that keeps you alive out here is trust. Break that trust and you die," Belinda said seriously.

"Okay, okay."

†

The first session with the psychologist was hard on Eric. He was withdrawn and jumpy and it broke Barbara's heart every time he jumped at the slightest noise. How could he not be afraid? She asked herself. He was just a little boy who had gone through something really horrible. And if not for Taya, it might have been even worse.

"Hey, how about we do takeout tonight?" Barbara tried to sound excited for him. She was fighting her own demons as well. For some reason she felt something ominous in the air.

"Chinese?" he asked hopefully.

"You got it," she said with a smile. "Go ask your brother what he wants and we will call in the order, okay?"

"Okay, Mom."

Taya suddenly came to mind again. She hadn't had a chance to talk to Taya about Jeff. She was going to when Taya was leaving but all that she could think of at the time was getting her not to go back to that place.

Taya, where are you? Barbara was suddenly filled with fear. She hadn't wanted to discuss Jeff coming over on the phone with her. Talking to Taya face-to-face seemed best. She would reassure her and Taya would understand. Right now all she could hope for was that Jeff would leave before Taya came back. Jeff rarely stayed long. Taya would understand. She would explain.

†

Jeff walked into the house as if he still lived there, two hours later than expected.

"Dad!" Sean yelled.

Barbara looked up from the sofa in the family room as he walked in through the door. She was about to say something to him when she thought better of it. Later, I'll talk to him about it later. She had to break this cycle of Jeff thinking he could just walk into the house unannounced.

Sean ran into Jeff's arms while Eric remained quiet in her arms as he sat with her watching cartoons.

Jeff looked at Eric then at Barbara. It was obvious that the boy had not looked at him at all.

"Hey, sport," Jeff said as he knelt down in front of him. "I'm glad to see you're okay."

Eric looked at him without saying a word. Jeff looked at Barbara, who was visibly concerned.

"I'm here, Eric." He went to tousle the boy's hair and Eric pulled away and went deeper into his mother's arms.

"Hey, buddy," Jeff said softly.

"Sweetheart, it's okay," Barbara tried to reassure him.

Eric hid his face in his mother's neck.

"What's wrong with him?" Jeff asked.

"He's just scared. It's okay, baby." Barbara held her son tighter to her.

Jeff sat down next to him. "Eric, wanna play some ball?"

Eric said nothing.

Barbara looked at Jeff. This was something that was unexpected.

"Eric, baby, we love you," Barbara said as tears began to fill her eyes.

Jeff put his hand over Barbara's.

Eric's head suddenly popped up.

"Eric?" Barbara looked at her son perplexed.

The front door opened and closed and within seconds Taya stood in the doorframe of the family room in all her glory. Her eyes immediately went to Jeff's hand over Barbara's.

Eric immediately ran into open arms that pulled him into a tight embrace.

"It's all right. You're safe, my son," Taya said softly into his ear but loud enough to be heard. "You're safe, Eric." She kissed his cheek softly.

Eric clung to Taya as if to his life force. "Where did you go?" he asked sulkily.

"I had some errands to run. You're safe, my little man," Taya reassured him again and kissed him on the head as she still held him in her arms. She turned to face Jeff and Barbara.

Jeff got up suddenly. Barbara looked from Taya to Jeff and back to Taya again. Taya knew instinctively who he was and seemed to stand taller. Two sets of eyes clashed.

"Eric, come here," Jeff said a bit too loudly.

Eric clung harder to Taya who held him tighter still. Barbara watched as Taya's dark eyes became something she had never seen before. Jeff must have seen it too because he took a step back.

"Eric, I brought you something. It's on the kitchen table." Taya's eyes were as cold as ice as they looked at Jeff but her voice was soft and tender to Eric. She put him down and tousled his hair. "Sean, I brought something for you too." Taya smiled toward the other boy.

Both children left the room, leaving Jeff and Taya facing each other. Barbara stood up quickly.

"This is Taya, Jeff. She found Eric. We owe her his life," Barbara said as she stood in front of Jeff. She could feel that tidal wave coming.

Taya took a few more steps into the room. Before her stood the man who, by all accounts, never knew how to take care of his family. All the dormant emotions inside her began to stir and the old anger at her own father started to build, and not only that, but this was her family now. He'd had his hand on…Barbara is mine! Isn't she? No one will take her from me! No one! The undercurrent of rage was visible in her eyes now.

Jeff looked from Barbara to Taya. Jeff knew enough to know that she was no ordinary woman. Taya was something wild and dangerous and she had walked into the house just like he had a few minutes before, like she belonged there, like she had a claim to his family.

"I want to reward you for what you did for my son." Jeff reached into his pocket and was about to take out a checkbook. Barbara turned to face him in disbelief. Everything was spiraling downward faster than she could stop it from happening.

"You're insulting," Barbara said in disgust.

"I'm sure, Miss… Jeff waited for Taya to speak and heard nothing from her.

"Jeff!" Barbara was mortified.

"You don't have enough money," Taya said between her teeth, barely able to control the anger inside her now.

"I bet I do." Jeff handed her a check as his eyes admired her body.

Barbara watched Taya as she took it and looked at it. Taya smiled.

"Ten thousand dollars," Taya said as she continued to stare at it. "Is that what your son is worth?" Taya looked up slowly. "I have more than this in petty cash." She ripped the check and let the pieces fall to the floor.

"You do, huh?" Jeff smirked.

"What are you worth?" Taya sat down while never losing eye contact at him. She was like the beast playing with what was about to be devoured.

Standing should have made Jeff feel taller, bigger, more in control but somehow it didn't. "Are we going to compare portfolios?" Jeff let out a laugh.

"I don't think so," Taya said indifferently.

Jeff had a smirk of satisfaction on his face as he looked toward Barbara.

"I don't think you would even come close," Taya said as her eyes challenged him.

"Right," Jeff said sarcastically.

"Is this a pissing contest, Mr. Williams? Because if you want one…"

"Taya! Please." Barbara took a few steps toward her.

"Who the fuck is this, Barbara? What the hell are you bringing home these days?" Jeff grabbed Barbara by the arm and before he knew it Taya stood in front of him with a switchblade on his neck. He felt the cold steel ever so lightly and yet knew that with just one twitch of her wrist he could be dead.

Everything was suddenly still. The only sound was Jeff's harsh breathing. No one moved and when Taya's low voice was heard it seemed to be as ominous and as deadly as the blade on his neck. Barbara seemed to be the only bridge of safety between them. One wrong move and Jeff knew as sure as he stood there that Taya would slit his throat.

"Don't you ever touch her…ever," Taya said softly between her teeth. "Not ever."

Jeff felt the blade push slightly into his skin.

Jeff let go of Barbara and his arm dropped slowly to his side.

Taya still had the blade to his neck.

Barbara stood between them barely able to breathe with fear. Her body swayed closer to Taya.

"Taya, please," Barbara implored. "Please, Taya. The boys may come in. Please, darling."

Jeff didn't flinch. He did not even blink for fear the movement would spook her.

"I beg you…" Barbara pleaded.

Taya took a step back and the blade disappeared into the inside pocket of her long leather jacket.

Jeff took a step back slowly and took a deep breath.

"I want you out of my house," Jeff said under his breath.

"This isn't your house." Barbara turned and faced him.

Jeff controlled himself because he had to. He looked toward Barbara. "Tell this woman to leave."

"No." Barbara took a step back and leaned against Taya.

"If you want a pissing contest I can arrange one," Taya taunted him with a malevolent smile.

"Taya." Barbara closed her eyes for a moment, praying that it would all just end.

Taya looked over Barbara's head at Jeff. Her arms went around Barbara's waist and pulled her back to her. "No one touches what's mine."

Jeff's face registered what he had just heard and understood what he saw.

"Yours?" Jeff said in disgust, refusing to believe the obvious.

"Don't push…I'm someone you don't ever want to push," Taya said as she took a step toward Jeff.

Barbara turned to face her and went into her arms to stop her.

"I want to kill you already," Taya growled softly. "Don't encourage me."

"Taya," Barbara looked up into a face she had never seen.

Jeff said nothing.

"Taya?" Barbara repeated. This woman in front of her was not her lover and that frightened her.

"Be nice to Eric and then get out. If you ever, ever do anything to hurt what is now mine…you won't live to see the next day."

Jeff stared at the face of death and believed every word she had uttered. Barbara also believed her. He took a step away from her and at that moment so did Barbara.

As Jeff walked past her to get to the door, Taya turned to Barbara with the same cold eyes. As Barbara looked into Taya's eyes, she realized those were the eyes she had seen that first night with Taya. Those were the eyes of the woman who had taken her that first night. Before her stood Black Angel.

"Taya?" Barbara said barely above a whisper.

Taya took Barbara into her arms and searched her face; when they stopped at Barbara's mouth it took barely a second before she claimed it.

The kiss was rough and possessive. Barbara tried to catch her breath only to be pulled deeper into the onslaught of the kiss. Taya released her only when she heard Jeff's voice from the kitchen. She walked out of the room leaving Barbara baffled and disturbed as to what had just happened.

✝

Barbara shook her head as if trying to wake up from a dream.

"Jeff!" She hurried after Taya, stopping dead in her tracks when she saw Taya with her arms crossed in front of her chest, leaning against the far wall of the kitchen, watching Jeff talk to the boys.

Barbara looked at Taya, then Jeff. He seemed more uncomfortable by the minute until he straightened up and began to say his goodbyes.

"Do you have to go, Dad?" Sean pulled at his sleeve.

"Yes, Sean, but I'll see you this weekend," he said, tousling the boy's hair.

148

"Can't you stay a little longer?" Sean tugged at his sleeve again.

Eric kept playing with his toy, trying to insert one piece into another, not participating in the conversation.

"No, Sean, I can't." Jeff's impatience, as usual, began to show.

Barbara asked herself how many times had this happened over the years and she had just taken over and smoothed the ruffled feathers between them. Had Jeff always been this impatient? Why couldn't he give the boys what they had always wanted most from him, his time.

Taya didn't miss a single expression on Barbara's face as she looked at Jeff.

Why does she look at him like that? Does she still love him? Taya shifted her weight from one foot to the other. Without saying a word she turned to walk out of the room, she couldn't bear to look at Barbara any longer. If Barbara was still in love with her husband she didn't have to see it so she started to leave.

"Where are you going?" Eric suddenly came to life.

Taya stopped, hearing the panic in the boy's voice. She turned toward him with the tenderest look Barbara had ever seen.

"I'll be back, okay?"

Eric smiled and nodded.

Jeff didn't miss a thing.

Eric followed Taya with his eyes lovingly as she walked out of the kitchen.

When Taya left the room Barbara's eyes turned and met Jeff's across the room.

"Well, boys, I have to go. I'll see you both on the weekend." He then leaned down to Eric. "I'm glad you're okay."

Eric nodded without looking at him.

Jeff got up and took a few steps toward Barbara. "We'll have to talk," he said to her and without saying another word he left.

✝

Barbara walked to the window and saw Jeff pull out of the driveway. Taya was nowhere to be seen. Barbara was worried. She thought she'd had a handle on things but she no longer believed that after what had happened in the family room. She didn't know what to think.

"Mom?"

Barbara turned around and saw Eric standing in front of her. He took a step closer and put his small hand in hers.

"She'll be back right?"

"Yes, darling. She said she would." Barbara smiled and kissed him.

"Okay."

Barbara looked out again and the fear and uncertainty covered her face again. *Taya, where are you?*

Chapter Twenty

Jeff pulled into his parking slot and got out of his car. He had bought the penthouse, in one of the most exclusive areas near Livingston, when he had moved out of the house. He liked leading the bachelor's life. He told himself he deserved to experience all that life had to offer. Barbara and he had married when they were young; Jeff told himself that he could have a wife and keep doing what he wanted—until Barbara found out about Veronica. Then it had all fallen apart. In the beginning he had convinced her that they should work on keeping their marriage together for the boys, but after a while she didn't believe him anymore. And now…now Barbara was with…

Jeff slammed the door to his car hard. "Fuckin' bitch!"

He would get Barbara back he told himself. After leaving Barbara he realized that Veronica was not the right woman for him. Barbara was his wife, the mother of his sons, and she was the only woman, he had to admit, who had touched his heart. Taya was her mistake, like Veronica was his. Barbara loved him. She would take him back. He knew her enough to know that her loyalty and her love of the boys would ensure that. She was, after all, his wife; Sean and Eric were his children. Through the boys he would get her back. He would challenge her custody of them if need be; that would make her come crawling back to him if all else failed.

The audacity of that thug to threaten me! The more he thought about Taya's threat the angrier he became. Jeff never saw the two men approaching until they were both standing in front of him.

He stopped dead in his tracks and stared from one to the other. Jeff took a step back then turned around only to see two more men close behind him.

"Nice and easy," one of the men said.

"What do you want?" Jeff felt every pore in his body fill with fear.

The men stared at him without uttering a word.

"What do you want?" he asked again, looking from one to the other. "You can have it all."

They still said nothing.

"Here, take it." Jeff pulled out his wallet and offered it to them along with his car keys.

They remained silent and unmoving. The seconds seemed like hours. His nerves began to crack and he began to visibly perspire.

Jeff heard footsteps and he desperately turned toward the sound. Then he saw her. She walked slowly toward them. It was her! Her long black coat flew up as a gust of cold air went through the parking lot. She approached, all clad in black, like a rider announcing imminent death. Jeff experienced fear like he had never felt before in every nerve ending.

Taya stopped a few feet away from him. All four men took a few steps back.

"I know who you are," she said, taking as step closer. "I know where you live." Another step, her voice remained soft and malevolent. "I know who you fuck," she said to him as she stood right in front of him. She tilted her head from side to side as those do when they are about to strike.

Jeff opened his mouth and was about to say something when he received a blow to his gut that bent him over. He groaned in pain, holding his stomach and trying not to fall down.

"I didn't ask you any questions," Taya said coldly. "You talk when an answer is required or you do not talk at all. If you understand now you may say yes." Her voice had an element of softness to it.

His mind was suddenly filled with a vision of darkness. Jeff felt himself surrounded and immersed in a warm liquid and horror filled his senses, his mind visualized what it was...it was blood. He could see it. He could taste it in his mouth. His eyes looked at Taya in horror. Her voice was the herald that was announcing his future...her words meant blood...warm blood, death.

Jeff barely straightened up, still trying to catch his breath. "Yesss..."

Taya took a step closer to him. He could feel her breath on his face. The same razor blade that had been on his neck an hour earlier was close to his face, caressing him. He felt the cold of the metal as it traveled down his cheekbone.

Taya's mouth was barely a whisper away as her eyes looked into his menacingly.

"You put one finger on my..." Taya's mouth twisted into a smile as he recognized who she was talking about. "Yes, she's mine."

Jeff felt the blade as it traveled down his throat now.

"I know her smell and her taste."

Jeff blinked nervously and his breath came in short breaths.

"Who does she belong to, Jeff?" Taya asked, getting even closer to him. He could feel her body pressed against him and suddenly he felt the blade once more. He hardly dared breathe as he felt the pressure of the blade increasing in his crotch.

"Oh God, please, don't." He let out a moan.

"Say it."

"She's yours," he blurted out quickly.

"Say it again." Her cheek rubbed his menacingly. Her eyes were closed as she did this…savoring her prey.

"She's yours. She's yours," Jeff repeated, whimpering.

"Remember that. Always remember that." She was looking straight at him now.

Jeff didn't feel the pressure lessen so he dared to look into her eyes again.

"I won't touch her ever again, I swear."

Taya took a step back and he fell to his knees in fear.

"Get up!" she growled.

Jeff got up and she looked down and smiled. In fear he had wet his pants.

"I won't stop you from seeing the boys. But don't make me come looking for you. Do you understand? If you hurt them I'll kill you."

Jeff nodded.

"Be nice to them."

Jeff nodded again.

Taya stepped closer and he began to look nervous again.

"I will always know where you are, Jeff…who you're with…what you do…all it will take is for me to raise one finger and…"

Sweat was running down Jeff's face.

Taya turned and walked away, leaving him surrounded by the four men.

"Remember what Black Angel said, mister, because if you don't I'm the last face you will ever see."

Jeff breathed hard through his nose trying to control his fear. He stood without moving a muscle as all four men walked away from him in different directions.

The only man who had spoken to him turned around again and pointed at him. "Remember." Then he disappeared into the shadows as well.

Jeff began to shake uncontrollably as he knelt down to pick up his wallet and his keys.

†

Taya was pumped. She hadn't felt this exhilarated in a long time. The animal in her had come to life as she roared her entrance into the pens. Heads turned as they heard the growling of her machine as she rode by.

She liked what she had done to Jeff Williams. She thought she would experience an orgasm from the pleasure of watching him fall apart in front of her. Taya licked her lips and tasted her victory. She then turned her bike toward the cage.

The cage was where men still fought with their fists. It was bloody and it was real. When Taya walked in all turned to her and showed their respect by subtly acknowledging her presence. As always a few of her men, who were always present, closed ranks around her.

Taya breathed in the smell of sweat and blood and smiled. This was her world and here her word was law. The night was still young. She saw Christopher on the far end with some of his girls.

Good, she told herself.

Not only would she have a piece of the purse; but she would have a take of the flesh market as well. Nothing ever happened in the pens without her having a piece of it.

A set of eyes watched as she walked in. Taya took a drink from a bottle offered. She laughed hard. The same set of eyes became saddened as they turned away from her and walked away. Belinda never looked back.

†

It had taken a while for Eric to fall asleep but it had finally happened. Barbara had finally managed to reassure him that Taya would come back. She had gone to bed but been unable to sleep, tossing and turning, worrying about Taya, until finally the strain of the day made her close her eyes.

Barbara awoke to hands touching her. She turned into the arms of her lover then smelled the alcohol in Taya's breath.

"Taya?"

Before Barbara could speak her mouth was covered roughly with Taya's, demanding a response.

"You belong to me," Taya said possessively.

Barbara could barely see her face but there was something about the touch of her lover that she didn't recognize.

"Darling?"

Taya pulled her roughly to her knees and began to remove Barbara's negligee.

Barbara reached out to touch her. She felt the warmth of her skin and her arms slid down lower in a caress until…

Barbara pulled away and stared, trying to see in the dark.

"What…?" Barbara asked in confusion.

"I want you," was all Taya said as she turned her around.

"Wait..." Barbara was suddenly turned around and was on her hands and knees.

"I want you," Taya growled.

"Taya…" Barbara said in fear and felt Taya hesitate.

"Are you mine?" Barbara heard the uncertainty of Taya's voice.

It was a simple question and yet it wasn't. Barbara had heard anger and she had heard love…and the reality of what Taya had actually asked her bathed her consciousness with fear and resignation. Taya needed this. Barbara let her head drop as she said, "Yes."

She waited for the piercing pain she knew would come but rather felt hands on her hips, holding them tightly in place. She shut her eyes tightly as she felt the penetration.

Taya breathed in deeply. Her nostrils still smelled the sweat and the blood of the cage. The blood coursing through her felt hot and she let out a guttural growl of pleasure as Black Angel was allowed to take her pleasure from the woman in front of her.

Barbara tried to pull away but Taya grabbed her by the hair with one hand as the other grabbed her shoulder and pulled her back toward her. She fucked Barbara even harder, reveling in the hedonistic pleasure she felt with every thrust into Barbara. She never heard Barbara continually saying her name as she wept.

A white ball of heat filled Taya with pleasure as she thrust into Barbara one final time and screamed her release. Taya breathed in deeply, satisfied. Only then did she hear Barbara sobbing. She pulled out of Barbara and let go of her hips. Barbara's pain had finally touched her.

Taya was suddenly filled with visions of what she had done. She had ridden her anger on Barbara's body. She had pulled Barbara's hair back, holding her in place, and Barbara had allowed it. This realization shocked her. She had taken it all out on the woman that, out of love, had allowed this violation of her body to satisfy her need. And to her shame Taya still felt it was not enough. The animal in her that had taken years to create would not be silenced. Not yet.

Taya took a step back, trying to distance herself as Barbara curled up and wept in bed.

"Ah…" it was more than a cry, more like the sound of a wounded animal that came out of Taya's mouth.

What have I done? Stop! Stop! What have I done? The screaming would not stop in her head. Feed Taya, feed and shut out the fire.

Barbara stared at Taya with a tear-stained face and saw Taya's horrified look. They regarded each other for a moment without speaking or breathing.

Taya's hand reached out to Barbara. She seemed to bend over in pain, her demons all too present in her face to hide as tears began to fall down her own face.

Barbara stared at the woman who had just used her and realized that she and Taya were one and the same. Who would win in the end? With tear-filled eyes she saw her lover still wanted more.

"Barbara…" Taya took a step closer. Barbara looked down at the leather straps and the dildo still attached to it. She held back a sob; she ached inside from the way that Taya had taken her. But when Taya covered her body again she didn't push her away. Barbara wept and opened her legs as Taya took her once more.

This time Taya was on top of her and when she entered her it was not as hard. Barbara tried touching her but Taya grabbed her arms and pinned her down. Taya buried her face into her neck and breathed harder as she kept going in and out of Barbara. As she let go of Barbara's hands to better ride her, Barbara wept silently as she held Taya tighter to her.

Taya collapsed on top of her, this time making Barbara come before she allowed herself the pleasure. Taya did not move. She stayed on top of Barbara. After a few moments Taya raised herself and met Barbara's eyes and kissed the tearful face then lay her head down again. She liked having Barbara under her like this she told herself. She liked being between her legs, knowing that Barbara was hers, and only hers. No one would touch her again. And that was the way it would be. No one would feel this. No one! Barbara was hers.

Barbara held her tightly not daring to think about what she had done. She was filled with love and pain and at the moment could not tell them apart. Taya lay on top of her. She felt her weight and the possessive way in which her hands held her.

What happened? Oh God, help me. Barbara wept silently as she kissed Taya's face and held her tighter. We can't live like this. God, not like this.

"I love you," Taya whispered into her hair. A sob escaped her as her body began to shake uncontrollably. "I love you," she repeated as her sobbing got louder. She felt Barbara's arms tighten around her, holding her, kissing her and caressing her. Barbara would caress the demons away; she was the only one who could…at least for another day. Tears mingled in the night as two souls clung together, one for sanity the other for hope.

Chapter Twenty-One

Taya woke up in bed alone. Her eyes hurt as she tried looking around the room. She lay back with a splitting headache. She covered her eyes with her arm and groaned. She tried sitting up but the room wouldn't stop spinning. After an hour or so she tried sitting up again and this time found the room remained still. Her hand went to her side. Her wound hurt. When she pulled back the covers to crawl out of bed her eyes widened as she saw the harness she still had on. All the events of the night came rushing into her brain with the fierceness of a hurricane.

"Barbara…" she murmured as she stood and pulled at the leather straps to remove the harness. It fell to the floor and she fell back on the bed again, her legs like jelly.

Taya stared for a moment without seeing. She breathed in deeply and closed her eyes as her head dropped back.

"Oh, my god…what have I done?" The horror of what had happened and what she had done to the woman she was supposed to love and protect filled her with dread and despair. The silence of the room began to stifle her. She had to find Barbara.

Taya wrapped the sheet around herself and on wobbly knees walked out of the bedroom. She called out Barbara's name when she stepped out into the hallway and received no response. She walked down the stairs slowly, hanging on to the banister, and found the lower floor empty as well. Her eyes wildly looked around in desperation.

✝

"Hi," said Barbara, walking into her sister's kitchen, after dropping the boys at school.

"Hi…what happened to your face?" Dale exclaimed, walking over to her sister for a hug.

"Would you believe I fought the car and lost?" Barbara joked.

"Are you serious?" Dale said, turning her sister's face to take a better look.

"How? When?" Dale inquired suspiciously.

"Yesterday. The car door swung open and I almost landed on my rear from the shock," Barbara explained as she pulled her face away from Dale's hand. "Got any coffee?" she asked as she sat down facing her sister.

Barbara looked at Dale and waved her hand in front of her eyes, trying to get a reaction.

"Earth to Dale," Barbara joked as she waved her hand at her sister again.

Dale's semblance remained serious. "You would tell me if…"

"Tell you what?" Barbara asked innocently. She knew exactly what her sister was thinking.

"Taya…" Dale trailed off.

Barbara got up quickly to reassure her sister. "No…Taya loves me. She…" Barbara ran her fingers through her hair and looked into her sister's vigilant eyes. "Taya is very capable of…but no, she would never intentionally hurt me. It was as I said, Dale." Her eyes filled with tears as she spoke.

Dale rushed over to her sister and embraced her. "I'm sorry…I just don't want anything to hurt you."

Barbara clung to her sister. "I know. I know." She had not lied she reasoned. Taya hadn't meant to hurt her last night.

"I just worry, Barb. Forgive me?" Dale said, looking at her sister now.

"Yes, I understand." Barbara wrapped her arms around herself, retreating a few steps away from Dale. "I do…I know that you love me, sis."

"I guess Taya's world is scary to me…I don't want to see you get hurt."

"Yes, it's hard to understand…" Barbara said softly.

"How are you two? I mean are you making any long-term plans?" Suddenly exasperated, Dale just downright asked what she was thinking. "Is she planning on changing her lifestyle?"

Barbara stared at her sister, at a loss for an answer.

"Well?" Dale sat down and waited. Something was up and she knew it.

"I…I guess we really haven't…"

"Don't you think you should?"

Barbara nervously ran her fingers through her hair. "So much as happened…we haven't really had a chance to talk yet."

"Barbara…"

"Taya loves me," Barbara affirmed.

✝

Barbara walked into the house, preoccupied with her sister's questions.

"Where were you?"

Barbara dropped her keys from the surprise.

Taya walked up to her and knelt down, picking up the keys and placing them back in her hands as she got up. Barbara took the keys nervously.

"I'm sorry I should have left a note, darling," she spoke as she walked to the kitchen.

Taya stood without moving as Barbara walked past her. It took all her resolve not to fall apart when she saw the bruise on the side of Barbara's face. She shut her eyes then took a deep breath, trying to control her emotions.

Barbara was pulling something out of the refrigerator when Taya came up behind her and held on to her tightly.

Barbara closed the refrigerator door and turned around quickly in Taya's arms.

"I'm sorry…" Taya said into her hair as she held Barbara tightly. "I'm sorry…"

Taya pulled away and looked at Barbara's face. Her eyes stopped at the bruise on her cheek. She caressed her face softly. "I shouldn't have been so rough."

"What happened?" Barbara asked somberly as her eyes searched Taya's face for an answer.

"What do you mean?" Taya answered defensively.

"You weren't making love to me."

"Who was I with then?" Taya pulled away from her, putting distance between them. "It's not the first time I've fucked you."

"Why are you angry?" Barbara didn't understand why Taya was acting like this.

"I said I was sorry, Barbara," Taya said as she walked out of the kitchen.

Barbara followed her into the living room.

"Are you?"

"Am I what?" Taya was becoming agitated as she paced.

Barbara stared at the woman she only thought she had imagined. Taya was changing before her very eyes.

"Sorry."

Taya faced her. "I'm sorry for the bruise, Barbara." She made it quite clear what she was apologizing for.

They stared at one another without speaking.

Taya could clearly see the doubts fill Barbara's face.

"Is this the part where you tell me that we are too different and should just call it a day?"

"What are you talking about?" Barbara took a step closer.

"You have to be the best piece of... I have enjoyed being with you, Barbara," Taya said as her face became unreadable.

Barbara stared at her in disbelief. "Why are you saying this?"

"Because it's time we call it a day. I gotta go," Taya said as she turned and began to walk away.

"You said forever..." Barbara said softly.

Taya froze, her back to Barbara. "Sometimes, forever is not possible.

"It is when two people love each other, Taya. I love you." Barbara knew something had really pushed Taya beyond what she was capable of handling and thinking that made her even more afraid. Taya was scared. She was really scared.

"It would never work, Barbara. I am what I am." Taya turned around quickly, anger visible in her face. "You aren't woman enough for the pens and I can't live here with you."

"Why?" Barbara asked softly as tears ran down her face.

"Because this is who I am. Look at your face, Barbara. That's what I am." Taya waited.

Barbara touched her cheek. "This is not who you are."

Taya turned away from her in exasperation. "That's the way I fuck, Barbara. That's the woman you met that night in the pens. That's..."

"That's not the woman who made love to me…not the one who saved Eric…not the one who almost died saving him. That's not the woman who played video games and laughed with all the joy of innocence. That's not the woman whose eyes promised to love me forever. That's not you, Taya!" Barbara finished angrily.

Taya lunged at her and grabbed her arms roughly. "You don't learn do you?" she growled.

"I see you, Taya…I see who you are. You may not like it but I do. You can't hide from me, my love. I see you," Barbara insisted.

Taya grabbed her hair with one hand and placed her other hand between Barbara's legs. "This is fucking…that's all it is."

"I love you…"

"Liar!" Taya released her and took a few steps away. "Liar! I saw how you looked at him. Liar!"

"At who?" Barbara stared at her in confusion.

"I almost killed him…I wanted to…" Taya said eerily.

"Are you talking about Jeff?" Barbara said in disbelief.

Taya stared in silence.

"No, I love you," Barbara insisted as she took a step closer to Taya. "I professed my love for you in front of him, in front of Dale. I will say it in front of the whole world if that is what will convince you. I love you, Taya. I fell in love with you from the very first moment," Barbara said as she looked into Taya's eyes.

Barbara could see the war raging in Taya's eyes.

"I want a life with you. I want a life of softness and beauty. I want this and so much more, my love." Barbara now stood in front of Taya. "I know that you want this too…I know you, my love."

"Barbara…"

"I want all the tomorrows of my life to be spent with you by my side."

"I…"

"I want to build a life with you away from all this. I want a chance to live a long and happy life with you, Taya." Barbara's hand slowly went up and caressed her face.

Taya's eyes closed and when she opened them Barbara saw them fill with tears.

"Barbara…oh god, Barbara, forgive me. I love you," Taya said as she fell to her knees and wrapped her arms around Barbara's waist.

Barbara caressed Taya's dark head of hair. "I love you."

Taya looked up. "I will change, Barbara. I will do anything. I need you, Barbara. I will do anything." Taya got up and took Barbara roughly into her embrace. "Don't ever leave me."

"Taya…oh Taya." Barbara cried with her.

"We'll go away. I'll do anything…anything."

✝

Taya and Barbara were sitting on the sofa in the family room. Barbara was holding Taya tightly in her embrace. How could someone so strong be so vulnerable? Taya was so fragile. She tightened her embrace and heard Taya's breath as she went deeper into her arms.

Barbara was going over so many things in her mind. It occurred to her that some of the conversation earlier was becoming too clear and portions of it must be looked at. Some misunderstandings needed to be cleared up quickly before they could grow and fester.

"Taya, why?"

Taya stirred and pulled out of her arms and stared straight ahead of her.

Chapter Twenty-Two

Taya stepped into her apartment and looked around. She threw her keys on a nearby table and shut the door behind her. Walking around the room she asked herself if there was anything here that really meant anything to her. There wasn't.

She went into her bedroom and headed for the closet. Inside she pushed open a hidden compartment and removed what she had come for. She took the box and went to sit on the bed to open it. When was the last time she had actually looked inside this box? It had been so long she couldn't even remember.

Taya separated the photos and a few envelopes. In this box was her life. Account numbers from Swiss bank accounts to overseas investments, contacts, routes and secrets that kept her alive. The photos caught her eye. She stopped to stare at an old photograph of an elderly woman. Her fingertips lightly touched the figure in the old photo, remembering the last words her mother had said to her over ten years before.

"Taya, vete! No quiero verte jamás. Vete!"

Taya closed her eyes as the old pain suddenly came to life inside her again. She had been shocked by her mother's words. She had expected recriminations but not banishment. Her mother had sealed her decision. Taya would never see her again. She had been set free and she ran. Taya had been running for years, the anger building and building till it had nowhere to go but at everything she touched. She didn't want to hear and didn't want to think. She wanted to only stop feeling.

With those words from her mother ringing in her ears Taya had run out the door and had kept running her whole life.

"Mamá! No!" Taya's sister had tried to go after her but her mother stopped her.

"She hears no one. I cannot control her anymore. I don't want to answer the door one day and have a policeman tell me that she is dead."

"Pero, Mamá." Her daughter began to cry.

"This way I won't know," the woman said sadly as her shoulders drooped and she walked away.

Taya briefly turned around and met her sister's eyes for a moment before she started running again.

✝

Taya pulled out her cell phone and keyed in a phone number. She waited patiently as the phone rang.

"*Oigo,*" a voice answered.

"Mamá…"

Taya heard a deep intake of breath.

"Mamá…"

"Taya?" She heard a voice ask barely above a whisper.

Taya felt the lump grow in her throat as a sob escaped her.

"Taya, mi niña, mi niña…" her mother wept.

"*Puedo verte?*" She had to ask humbly. Her mother had to be the one to decide whether to allow her back into her life.

"*Mi niña sí, estás bien? Dónde estás? Taya, te quiero mucho, mi niña, te quiero mucho,*" the elderly voice cried. In a few words Taya had heard all she needed to know and she openly wept. "*Ven, Taya, ven...*"

The sobbing racked her body as she heard the final word of 'come.'

"No llores, mi amor, no llores."

Her mother had softly said don't cry and all she could do was weep. She longed for the arms that as a child she had always felt around her in comfort. It was Barbara...she had given her back all this, Taya thought.

✝

A few hours later Taya again stood in the middle of the apartment and looked around. She had never truly lived here. She would not miss it. It was easy to walk out and close the door to it. The world of the pens, however, would be a totally different undertaking, but for her to survive now she would have to find a way to leave it behind.

She had taken the first few steps toward another life and for the first time in a long time she felt hopeful.

Taya walked out of the apartment building, put on her sunglasses and inwardly smiled. She jumped on her bike and rode out of the pens.

The only word to describe what she felt was elation. She pulled into Barbara's driveway and ran up the stairs, taking two steps at a time and ran excitedly into the house.

"Barbara!"

Barbara walked in from the family room. Taya took her into her arms and twirled her around the room as the air around them filled with laughter.

Taya finally put her down and with a smile still on her face said, "I love you, Barbara. I want the rest of my life to be with you."

Barbara was about to speak when Taya interrupted. "I called my mother," Taya said as her eyes filled with tears.

"And…?"

"She was so happy…I haven't called in over ten years. I want this life as much as you do, *querida*."

Barbara smiled and caressed Taya's face. Finally, she could see a glimmer of peace in those eyes looking back at her.

"I want her to meet you," Taya said excitedly.

"You told her about me?"

"I told her I met a woman who made me want to change my life," Taya said as her lips lightly kissed Barbara's.

"Taya, she may not…"

"She will love you, and the boys can use a vacation. Just think, Barbara, water, sand, sun, and a new beginning," Taya said excitedly.

"Don't you think that perhaps you should spend some time with your mother first?"

"This new life is because of you, *querida*. I will not spend another day without you in it," Taya said emotionally. She took Barbara's face between her hands and looked at Barbara for a moment before speaking, "*Te amo, te amo*…what I feel for you is stronger than love…you are my life, Barbara, my life."

†

Barbara had called Eric's therapist who thought the trip would actually be good for him. With that approval she started packing. When the boys got home they jumped with excitement. While Barbara packed she could hear them running with glee as Taya chased them around the rooms downstairs. Barbara smiled as she thought about how different Taya was now…that's all she allowed herself to think.

The next day they were getting in an airplane and flying toward Florida. Taya had gone out and come back the night before with four first-class tickets.

"Darling, I could have helped to pay for those," Barbara said carefully, not wanting to offend her lover in any way.

"Only the best for my family. Money is not something that we have to worry about," she had said simply then went to look for the boys. "Hey, guys, want to play Battle Star?"

Barbara watched now as Taya fussed over Sean and Eric. "You guys okay over there?"

"Darling, they are fine. You bought them enough games for the Gameboys to keep them enthralled for at least the foreseeable future," Barbara said, smiling. She would have to talk to Taya about all the presents. She didn't want to discourage her from her attentiveness, but she didn't want her to be constantly buying the boys presents either. It just wasn't good for them. There would be time for that discussion she thought to herself and smiled. There was a lifetime to spend with Taya now.

"Are you happy?" Taya covered Barbara's hand with her own.

"I have you. Yes."

Taya's smile had never seemed brighter.

✝

"Taya, come on, I want to go down to the beach!" Sean insisted.

Taya stepped out of the bedroom and smiled indulgently at the boy. "Can't wait, huh?"

"Please…" Sean looked at her in the way he knew she could never said no to.

171

"Okay, grab a towel. Let me tell Mom that she can meet us downstairs with Eric, okay?"

"Okay..." Sean said excitedly.

Taya turned around and smiled sheepishly as she saw Barbara leaning against the doorframe with her arms crossed over her chest. "Pushover," Barbara said with a smile.

"Would you mind?" Taya nodded and smiled.

"No, go ahead. When Eric is ready I will meet you both downstairs." Barbara walked up to her slowly and stood in front of her. They were still careful in front of the boys.

"Come on, Taya, just kiss Mom and let's go pleaseeeee..." Sean whined.

Barbara and Taya stared at the boy then back at each other.

"You kiss her, Mom," Sean again insisted.

It had happened that simply. Barbara leaned up and kissed Taya lightly on the lips.

Taya, just as stunned, left the suite with Sean by the hand.

"You okay with this, little man?"

"With what?" he said as he looked up at her.

"With me and your Mom?" Taya asked tentatively.

He stopped suddenly and looked up at her. "Yeah, I'm okay with it. Eric and I had a long talk about it." He started walking again and Taya felt as if she was being walked instead of the other way around.

"You and Eric?"

"Yeah."

"I love you all more than anything, you know," Taya said simply, too choked up with emotion to say anything else.

"I know," the child simply said as they continued to walk down the hall toward the elevator.

✝

They had decided to stay at a hotel for a few days before going to meet Taya's mother. Taya felt more than saw Barbara's worries. She wanted it to work. All that she had done would not be allowed to touch the woman she loved. They had a chance, a real chance, at building a life together and she was prepared to do anything to make that happen.

They boys loved that the hotel they had chosen to stay at was right on the water. The Fontainebleau boasted to being one of the most luxurious places on the strip. Barbara had again suggested that she help pay for the accommodations but Taya had just smiled and said no.

Once they were upstairs and all settled in, the real meaning of what they had just begun hit Barbara.

"Taya?" Barbara had tentatively reached out to her lover after the boys were in their bedroom on the other side of the suite.

"Yes, *querida*." Taya turned to face her.

"We really haven't made any plans, have we?" Barbara looked deeply into her eyes. "I think we should, don't you?"

Taya walked up to her slowly. "Loving you for the rest of my life is my plan."

Barbara smiled but would not be deterred. She looked toward the bedroom where she heard the boys giggling.

"I love them too, Barbara," Taya said reassuringly.

"I know you do," Barbara said as her hand caressed the face of the woman in front of her. "But, there are things that we must discuss."

Taya pulled away suddenly. "What?"

Barbara came up behind her and wrapped her arms around her softly. "The little things that will make our future."

"I don't understand," Taya said as she turned around and again put distance between them.

"Taya, there are things I need to know," Barbara tried to explain.

"All you need to know is that I love you." Taya quickly took her into her arms.

"Taya…" Barbara's mouth was covered with lips that hungrily took her.

"Mom?"

Both women turned around. Barbara headed toward the boys' room. Taya stared as she walked away. Barbara stopped and turned back to her. "I will be back once I put them to bed."

Taya nodded.

Once alone she went into the bedroom they would share and stepped out onto the balcony. Barbara had questions she told herself. It was natural for her to have questions. Taya, however, knew that the answers might be very hard to swallow. She had been dreading this moment from the first time she realized that Barbara was the woman that she loved and needed in her life. Now the questions were here and she was more afraid than she had ever been in her life.

Barbara found Taya out on the balcony and came up behind her and leaned her head on her back. "Come to bed. I need you."

Taya turned around and kissed her with desperation.

"Do you?" Taya voiced in the darkness as the woman she loved stood in front of her.

"Do I what, darling?"

"Need me?"

Barbara took the step that separated them and put her arms around Taya's neck as she pulled her mouth down to her own before saying, "More than life itself."

"Are you worried about seeing your mom?" Barbara asked softly, feeling Taya's vulnerability not only in her speech but also in the silences of what was not said.

Taya turned toward the view off the balcony, avoiding Barbara's eyes. "A little I guess."

Barbara kissed her bare shoulder lightly. "She will love seeing you."

"I hope so, *querida*, I hope so."

✝

The next morning they all got into the limo that the Fontainebleau provided for some of their guests. The boys jumped in, giggling with excitement as they moved from seat to seat.

"Boys, settle down," Barbara said.

"It's okay, they're just excited," Taya said indulgently.

"Sweetheart, you spoil them."

"I like it," Taya said as she lovingly looked at the boys.

"Hmmm…" She then directed her comment at her sons again. "I want you both on your best behavior when we meet Taya's family, okay?"

"Okay, Mom," they responded in unison.

Taya smiled as they offered their mother their angelic faces.

✝

Taya got out of the car first, unable to wait for the chauffeur to come around. She clenched and unclenched her hands, a sign Barbara knew too well that she was trying to hide herself from the world.

Barbara stepped out of the car and slipped her hand into Taya's, and as she did felt Taya's hand tighten around hers.

175

The house was a modest one and the outside looked well taken care of. There was a warm breeze and the scent of roses was all around them.

"I missed that," Taya whispered to herself.

At that moment the front door opened and an elderly woman stepped out. She stared at Taya with such love that all the shadows that had filled Taya about this meeting dissipated. She ran into her mother's arms like a small child.

"*Mi niña...mi niña,*" she whispered into Taya's ear. Taya began to sob as her hold on the elderly woman tightened.

"*Mamá, Mamá, perdóname.*" Taya begged to be forgiven.

"*Nada importa, mi niña, nada importa.*" Her mother told her at that moment that nothing mattered and at that moment it didn't.

"Is this your family?" her mother asked as she directed her attention to Barbara and the two boys.

"Yes, Mamá, this is Barbara." Her mother did not miss the look that covered her daughter's face.

At that moment she opened her arms to Barbara, who without hesitation stepped into them.

"You are beautiful," Taya's mother said as she released Barbara looked at her in admiration from arm's length. "Welcome to our family."

"Thank you." Barbara's eyes appeared to water. "Thank you."

"And these two young men, these are your boys?"

"Yes," Taya interrupted before Barbara could answer. "These are our boys, Mama, Sean and Eric."

Taya's mother stared into her daughter's eyes and nodded in understanding. The whole exchange did not go unnoticed by Barbara.

"*Hola, abuelita,*" both boys greeted her in Spanish.

She smiled and took both boys by the hand and walked them into the house as Taya and Barbara followed.

"It is so good to have big and handsome grandsons. Your little cousins, Emily and Carla, will be here to meet you this afternoon with the rest of the family. I have treats that I made just for you," she said to them indulgently.

"*Flan abuela?*" Eric asked and Taya's mother could not help but laugh.

"I know who put you up to that."

Eric turned toward Taya. "I said it right, right?"

Everyone laughed as they walked into the house. The rest of the family would all be there to welcome them in the afternoon. Taya reached out for Barbara's hand just as Barbara's went out to meet it. She was truly home…at last.

Frozen, Black Angel Rising

By: S. Anne Gardner

Preview of Sequel to Cold and Lonely, Lovely Work of Art

A crash and the sound of breaking glass made a woman sit up quickly on the bed. The man lying next to her jumped out of bed and pulled out a handgun from the nightstand drawer.

"Rico?" The female voice was filled with fear.

Rico looked at his wife before the door to their bedroom burst open and the night was filled with gunfire. The last thing he saw was the face of the woman he loved and the red liquid that seemed to be covering her body. "Miranda!"

✝

"How could you think that I can live without you? Walk away, just walk away, Taya, please," Barbara begged in tears.

"I can't." It was the last thing she said before the she walked out.

Barbara fell to the floor like a rag doll that suddenly found she had no legs. She felt numb. Utterly numb…

All she heard in the distance was the roar of the beast as Black Angel rode toward the pens.

It had been foolish to think that she could just walk away. The pens and alliances had pulled her back in. There was a law in the pens and it had to be served.

Taya rode through the dark streets of a world that she knew, a world that she understood, a world that had been home for too long to leave behind just like that. Heads turned as she rode by and all knew that blood would be running in the pens soon.

All elements, good and bad, acknowledged her as their Queen. Black Angel was back in the pens and now the real war would begin. Word spread quickly and fear began to spread.

Black Angel pulled up to an old abandoned warehouse down by the Newark docks. Out of nowhere Christopher and Stanley came to meet her. They walked in together, no one uttering a word. They knew why they were there and as a united front they were perceived. At this moment numbers meant strength and mercy was weakness.

Rico walked toward her, still looking pale and wearing a sling that held his left arm in place. He was limping but the strength that kept him upright was the fire of hatred in his eyes.

She looked around the warehouse and saw what was left of his men and hers. They were arming themselves, getting ready to face what was the everyday of the pens, life and death. But this time it would be different. This time she would not be able to control the blood that would follow.

"You look like hell," Taya voiced out loud to Rico.

"I feel like hell."

"Where did we get the guns?"

"No need to ask…" Rico answered. "Word on the street is that they are going to be supplying the candy."

"Fucking optimistic aren't they," she growled then turned to Stanley. "Send some footmen, Stanley. I want to know how many there are."

Without another word Stanley took off.

"Christopher, I want information…" No explanation was necessary. Christopher was going to get his stables to dig.

"You got it, Taya."

Taya turned to Rico as Christopher walked away.

"I want to kill them all," Rico growled under his breath.

"Every single one, my friend."

†

Barbara heard the roaring of the motorcycle as Taya pulled into the driveway. She took a deep breath and realized that until that moment she had not known whether Taya would be coming back.

The boys had been long since asleep. Barbara looked toward her nightstand and saw the clock read 4:45 a.m. She heard the front door open and Taya coming slowly up the stairs. Her heart was pounding so hard that the sound of it became loud drums in her ears. Finally the door opened slowly; the moonlight coming through the window allowed her to see as Taya walked in.

Taya stood in the doorframe like a statue.

Barbara reached for the light switch on the lamp next to her. The room was bathed in a soft glow. As Barbara's eyes turned toward Taya she felt her breath freeze within her.

Taya was covered in blood and her eyes were more alive than she had ever seen them.

Barbara slowly got out of bed, never losing eye contact with Taya. She walked toward her and when she reached her took her by the hand. Taya followed.

She walked Taya to the bathroom and ran the shower. Not a word was spoken between them.

Taya's eyes followed Barbara with no emotion.

Barbara avoided her eyes and began to peel the clothes off Taya's body. They felt wet as she let them drop to the floor. Taya's body was covered with a film of blood.

Barbara removed her robe and gently pulled Taya into the hot shower with her. Taya did not speak. In silence Barbara washed her body and her hair clean. She then towel dried her. As she took Taya's hand she finally looked up to meet Taya's eyes.

Lifeless, Taya's eyes were now lifeless. The aliveness she had seen earlier was gone. A sob escaped her as she stepped into Taya's embrace and wept. She could no longer hold on to the fear that had filled her or the uncertainty of a life with her.

Barbara looked up and was met with Taya's lips. They kissed and exacted emotion. Taya's hunger came alive as her hands reached for the warmth of Barbara's body.

The sobbing had not ceased but Black Angel could not hear. She wrapped her strong arms around Barbara's body tightly and physically walked them both to the bedroom.

"Kiss me, kiss me…" Taya asked desperately as both bodies fell back onto the bed.

About the Author

S. Anne Gardner

S. Anne Gardner currently resides in the east coast of the United States, having lived and traveled all over the world. This brings her writing a clarity and realism that is unique among authors in the genre. She lives with her partner of many years who is a constant fountain of inspiration to her stories. Her sons fill her life with so much wonder and beauty that one way or another she finds ways of incorporating them in her work. She values her privacy and her family and friends are a part of a world that she has created for herself, nothing else is really required for her. She loves music, art, traveling and has a passion for writing and living life. Ms. Gardner lives in the details and knows these to be the ones that make up the tapestry of her life.

Other Books From Affinity eBook Press

HER—Lisa Ron

Fox has been looking for that one person who will make her feel complete-her perfect match.

Together with her friends, Megan and Tree, Fox continues her quest while dodging exes and clingers, laughing a lot along the way.

When she meets Madeline, she instantly knows that she finds HER.

Madeline has her own problems-notably a domineering husband.

Can Fox win her heart? Can they make a life together?

This story will make you laugh, cry, and hold your breath as the story unfolds.

With the right person love can conquer all.

Letting Go—JM Dragon   A failed relationship puts Stella Hawke's life on the brink of chaos.

When her grandmother falls gravely ill in Ashville, Stella ends her army career to take care of the woman during her last weeks. Little does she know that an old army comrade, socialite Reggie Stockton, whose family owns the local newspaper, also lives in Ashville.

Will she allow herself to accept Reggie's help to turn her life around and let go of the past?

This is a journey where both women re-evaluate what they want out of life.

Will that path lead to happiness or to a parting of the ways?

Private Dancer—TJ Vertigo Reece Corbett grew up on the mean streets on New York City, abused, used and in trouble with the law. Faith Ashford grew up wealthy, with all the creature comforts that money provides. When they meet fireworks begin.

Taming the Wolff—Del Robertson
ONLY ONE WOMAN...
As devastatingly beautiful as she is headstrong, noble-born Alexis DeVale abruptly finds her preordained life in upheaval. Abducted at swordpoint, held for ransom, thrust into a maelstrom of lawlessness and piracy...
HAS THE POWER...
The strength of her passion, the depth of her love...
TO TAME THE WOLFF...
Mayhem. Brutality. Murder. These are the tools of the trade - and Kris Wolff is the master of her profession. Captain of the high seas, a roguish pirate, her heart hardened by life, her passion tightly controlled by the secret she's forced to keep. Faced with a new danger, The Wolff finds herself unable to guard her heart from the tumultuous desires that Alexis DeVale has awakened.

Till There Was You—S. Anne Gardner
Julia is a woman used to power and is not afraid to use it or impose her will to get her way. She appears to have the world but a part of her is empty and cold as a frozen tundra. Julia rides in the mornings to clear her head and to make plans for what she is about to set in motion. Theodora, known as Teddy, is trying to put together a marriage filled

with uncertainties. She felt once upon a time that she would have a great love but that has eluded her. One morning these two women meet and from the first instance, it is explosive. The attraction is undeniable, the fears very real and the end without question will change them both forever.

Bayou Justice—Ali Spooner

Hell hath no fury like a woman scorned. When Kara, Sasha's, new lover is taken hostage as a diversionary tactic to allow the drug dealing Bellfontaine brothers to escape justice, Sasha springs into action.

Kara is released physically unharmed, however, her emotions, and budding career in the District Attorney's office are left in shambles when she is held blame for their release,

Appalled, by the failure of the criminal justice system, Sasha exacts her own brand of justice for the acts committed against her lover. From the Bayou's of Louisiana to the jungles of South America, Sasha plots her revenge.

Sugarland—Ali Spooner

Sasha Thibodaux travels to London from New Orleans to continue her studies as a concert pianist at King's College. While exploring her new home she befriends Milly Vansant, artist and instructor. When their friendship blossoms into love, Milly reveals her true nature as a vampire to Sasha who joins her in love for eternity. Their romance survives the tragic sinking of a luxury liner, during the Great War, a killer hurricane and the Spanish Flu pandemic as they travel back to the states to escape a war torn Europe. Sugarland, the plantation home they purchase as their home for eternity, or so they thought when tragedy strikes again.

Galveston 1900: Swept Away—Linda Crist

On September 7-8, 1900, the island of Galveston, Texas, was destroyed by a hurricane, or 'tropical cyclone', as it was called in those days. This story is a fictional account of Mattie and Rachel, two women who lived there, and their lives during the time of the 'great storm'. Forced to flee from her family at a young age, Rachel Travis finds a home and livelihood on the island of Galveston. Independent, friendly, and yet often lonely, only one other person knows the dark secret that haunts her. Madeline "Mattie" Crockett is trapped in a loveless marriage, convinced that her fate is sealed. She never dares to dream of true happiness, until Rachel Travis comes walking into her life. As emotions come to light, the storm of Mattie's marriage converges with the very real hurricane. Can they survive, and build the life they both dream of?

This second edition of one of Linda Crist's best-loved novels maintains the original story, while incorporating some reader-pleasing passages that were cut from the first edition. As an added bonus, the short story "Something to Celebrate" is included at the end of the novel, detailing further adventures of Rachel and Mattie.

Out of Retirement—Erica Lawson

Melanie Stokes was a doctor—a very good one, or so she hoped. She was calm and cool under pressure, and very little fazed her. Until…

Caitlin Joseph ran a small retirement home for older women in need. The fact that everyone in the house was gay was a coincidence, although it did cut down the number of women agreeing to live there.

Mel took up an offer to do some relief work for a local community center when their regular doctor was away on holidays. As soon as she arrived at the home she knew something was different about the place. Was it the little old lady chasing the paper boy down the street or the sign saying "Dykes Retirement Home"?

But there was something about the place that also appealed to her. Sure, Caitlin was cute as a button, but it was more the fact that she took very good care of her charges, despite their rather bizarre behavior.

The older women seized the opportunity to introduce a woman into Caitlin's lonely life, using any means possible to keep Mel coming back. Their plans were boosted by the introduction of another woman into the house, who set hearts a fluttering and blood pressure rising. Now if she was a lesbian it would have been perfect…

Denial—Jackie Kennedy

Time spent in Somalia has Doctor Celeste Cameron accustomed to living and working in a war zone. Coming back home to America, Celeste is glad to see the end of the peril she has been in—or so she thinks. Danger seems to follow Celeste and she finds it in the shape of Amy. What Celeste feels for Amy scares her more than anything she has faced in war zones. Amy has the same feelings, but is in denial and vows to marry Josh, Celeste's twin brother, no matter what. When fate brings them together again, will they give in to their mutual attraction or will they once again deny what they feel.

Bailey's Run—Ali Spooner

Bailey Chambers mourns the loss of her lover, Nessa, in an unsolved carjacking. When Tommy, Bailey's brother becomes a victim of a gay bashing, Bailey assumes his case will be handled the same way as her lover's—lackadaisically.

Desi Dexter assigned to Tommy's case, feels Bailey's disdain toward her and her partner. Through tenacious police work, Desi, is able to uncover the reason for Bailey's attitude, and convinces her that she is sincere in solving the case.

Mutual attraction sparks, and before they can move forward with their fledging romance, Desi, and her partner Braxton, uncover the presence of a serial killer.

What will happen to Bailey, when, Desi, becomes engrossed in another case, can their relationship survive?

Desert Blooms—Dannie Marsden

Luce's story continues in DESERT BLOOMS…

When we last met Luce Velazquez in Desert Heat, she went through hell and back to salvage her soul and reputation. Hoping to get her life back on track with lover Beth Ryan, a woman who understands her pain and can relate on every level. Instead, Luce is in the hospital, and Beth in protective custody.

Jessica Sullivan, Luce's friend and ex, has big doubts about the sincerity of Beth's love, and is in no hurry to release her from custody.

Can Luce's new found happiness last, or is Jessica correct in her doubts?

A heart stopping romance that will fill you with the wonder of friendship, anger of betrayal, and the everlasting vision of love.

E-Books, Print, Free e-books

Visit our website for more publications available online.

www.affinityebooks.com

Published by Affinity E-Book Press NZ LTD
Canterbury, New Zealand

Registered Company 2517228